Murder Behind the Coffeehouse

By

Brenda Kennedy

And

Kayden Keaton

***

Pineapple Grove Cozy Murder Mystery Series

Book 1

Synopsis

Piper thought that moving to a quaint town in Virginia would be the answer to her problems. Sunshine, fruity adult beverages, and white sandy beaches, but she never suspected murder would touch her new cozy community.

When a longtime resident of Pineapple Grove suspiciously dies, people suspect everyone, including Piper, who lives there, of murdering the defenseless woman.

Piper doesn't believe anyone in Pineapple Grove could be responsible for murdering the elderly woman. It's a small, tightknit community. Neighbors murdering neighbors doesn't happen here, does it? Who hated the longtime resident enough to want to kill her? She doesn't know, but she's determined to find out.

However, Piper quickly discovers not everything is as it seems. The small town is full of gossip, jealousy, and revenge. People you think are your friends aren't, and people you don't trust are maybe the ones you should.

Can Piper solve the murder with the help of her newfound friend and newspaper reporter, Lindsey Miles, before the killer strikes again? Or will this be another cold case murder?

ISBN: 9798548539717

Dedicated with love to Derek

This is a work of fiction. Names, characters, businesses, places, events, and incidents are either the products of the author's imagination or used in a fictitious manner. Any resemblance to actual persons, living or dead, or actual events is purely coincidental.

TABLE OF CONTENTS

CAST OF CHARACTERS

Piper Armstrong: Coffeehouse owner

Paul Armstrong: Piper's son

Hannah Armstrong: Piper's daughter

Mildred Moore: Town gossip (one of many)

Lindsey Miles: Newspaper reporter

Ethel Bowers: Town's old maid

Bob and Barb Stevens: The butcher and owner of the market

Bailey: Piper's poodle

Stephanie: The innkeeper

Alexander Abbott: Sheriff

Hunter Gallagher: Lindsey's photographer

Ruby Gallagher: Hunter's mother

Sally: Hairdresser

Liam Greer: Judge

Abigail Bowers: Ethel's sister

Harper Sinclair: Librarian

Carson Eubanks: Ethel's old boyfriend

Maverick Smoker: Pub owner

Jace Keck: New Deputy

Banks: Owner of The pub on the River

Amy: Banks' employee

Scott: Paul's friend

Polly: Owner of Polly Print Shop

CHAPTER 1

The ringing cell phone awakens Piper Armstrong. With her eyes still closed, she feels around the nightstand for her ringing phone. She knows without even looking that the caller is her only son, Paul. He's the only person to call her at this time of night.

Paul isn't happy with her choice of songs for his specific ringtone. She did it mostly as a joke, but after his last DUI, she decided the song was a perfect fit.

She swipes her finger across his photo icon, abruptly ending Elvis Presley's "Jailhouse Rock." "Hello," she groans.

"Mom, it's me," answers her twenty-three-year-old son. Paul is still trying to find his way in life. He still lives with Piper half of the time and stays with his friends the other half. When he's not at either place, you can find him in a 12x12 jail cell.

"What is it, Paul?"

"I need you to come get me."

"Come get you?" She peeks one eye open as she looks at the alarm clock on the nightstand. The big red numbers read 3:10 a.m. "Where are you, Paul? It's three in the morning. I have to get up in an hour. Can't it wait?"

"I'm in jail, Mom."

She isn't totally surprised, but she is disappointed. "Not again, Paul."

"I got pulled over coming home from Scott's house. We had a couple drinks. I fell asleep and when I woke up I wasn't drunk anymore and I wanted to come home. Well, I got pulled over and I still smelled like alcohol so they brought me to jail and charged me with driving under the influence of alcohol."

"Are you telling me they didn't do a breathalyzer test on you?" Paul doesn't answer. "That's what I thought. And let me guess, you didn't pass it? Which means, you were drunk."

"I didn't feel drunk."

"Paul, I..." Piper thinks about telling him to find another way home and to grow up and act his age, but she doesn't have the fight in her. Not this time of the night or morning.

"Mom, please," he pleads.

"Fine. I'll be there in a few," she says with irritation in her voice. She decides to save the lecture for when they're face to face and when she's more awake and he's less drunk.

She disconnects the phone and feels around the nightstand for her glasses. Putting them on she gets out of bed and heads to the bathroom to shower. *No need to rush. It's not like he's going anywhere.*

She showers and dresses for the day since she'll need to be at the coffeehouse to get it ready for what she hopes is another productive day.

Piper pulls up to the jail, pays his bond, and twenty minutes later, out walks Paul.

Paul gets into his mother's car and she drives him to her house before she heads a few blocks away to her coffee and doughnut shop: Bean There, Dunk That.

"I don't have to tell you how irresponsible this is, do I?"

"No, Mom. I already know."

"Then why are you repeating your mistakes?"

"I wasn't drunk."

"What did you get arrested for?"

"D.U.I."

"Driving under the influence. I rest my case. You shower and when you're done you walk over to the coffeehouse."

"I have to walk?"

"I don't have time to wait for you to get ready. You either walk or you can call Scott or an Uber. It's your money?"

"You expect me to work?" Piper glares at her son and with one glance it's like he can read her mind. He knows better than to argue anymore with her. After all, she is right. He woke her up out of her slumber and she went to bail him out without more than a few words. He knows that running a business isn't easy. It requires hard work, long hours, and much dedication. "I'll hurry."

Piper gets to the coffeehouse earlier than normal. Locking the door behind her, the first thing she does is make herself a small pot of coffee, then she starts baking the sweet cinnamon rolls her customers have grown to love. Next up, doughnuts. Lastly, she'll start the coffee for the customers.

Paul arrives at the coffeehouse at the same time as the first customer: Mildred Moore. He knows his mother won't be happy with him. One, for being arrested and going to jail, and two, for not being here to help her open the shop.

"Good morning, Paul," Mildred says as she makes her way to the front entrance.

At least someone's glad to see him.

"Good morning, Mildred. Let me help you with that," Paul says, reaching down to get Mildred's crocheting bag. When Paul bends down, Mildred smells the alcohol on his breath.

"Is that alcohol I smell?" Mildred asks. "You sure you're sober enough to be working?"

Paul sighs, blowing out a long breath and hoping it doesn't smell of the Jim Beam he was drinking a few hours earlier. "I'm not drunk, Mildred." *Not anymore*, he thinks to himself.

"If you say so. Just make sure you don't drop my bag."

"I promise I won't hurt your yarn," he mutters.

He picks up the bag and thinks it's heavier than it should be for containing yarn, patterns, and crocheting needles. But he says nothing. Maybe the bag contains more than crocheting items. Maybe Mildred has a drinking problem of her own. He lightly shakes the bag listening for a couple of alcohol bottles to clink together. Nothing. Maybe she isn't toting alcohol around after all.

Paul walks back to the kitchen just as another batch of bear claws come out of the oven, and he notices two more trays cooling. He washes his hands before putting on an apron. "Mildred's out there," Paul says to his mother.

Piper looks at Paul and decides she needs to have a responsible talk with her irresponsible son. It's tough love, but either he straightens up or some other changes will need to be made. She can't continue to run the coffeehouse by herself or with someone she can't rely on. Piper's hoping talking with him will be enough to straighten her son up and get him back on track. However, it wasn't enough the last time he did the exact same thing.

"Will you stock the doughnut case while I tend to Mildred?"

"Gladly."

Mildred's seventy-, maybe eighty-years-old. She's the first person to arrive and on most days she's the last person to leave. Mildred's also known by the locals as the town's busybody and gossip. If you want to know something, ask Mildred. She always sits at a two-top table by herself and contributes to every conversation within hearing range. Every morning, she orders one glazed doughnut in the morning, eats a peanut butter and jelly sandwich and a piece of fruit she pulls from her bag at lunch, and partakes in the free coffee refills until two o'clock when the coffeehouse closes for the day. At one time I thought about saying something to her about bringing food into my coffeehouse but then I decided why bother. If she doesn't have anywhere to go and she wants to stay here, what harm is a sandwich going to do.

While Paul stocks the glass serving case with doughnuts, Piper waits on Mildred. Although Piper already knows what Mildred wants, Mildred likes to be asked first. Piper waits patiently as Mildred pulls out her afghan, yarn, and crochet needle.

"What will you have this morning?" Piper asks.

Mildred smiles. "One glazed doughnut, not too much glaze. A coffee with a little cream and three sugars."

"Coming right up," Piper says, walking away.

"You should probably get a coffee for Paul, too," Mildred yells loud enough for Paul to hear. Piper glares at her adult son as she walks towards the self-serve coffee station. If Mildred knows he was arrested last night for a DUI, everyone in town will know before the day's over with. "It'll sober him up, but he'll need to drink it black and strong. The stronger the better, I'd say."

Paul yells from over the counter, "I'm not drunk, Mildred."

Once Mildred is served, Lindsey Miles walks in. Lindsey is the reporter for the local newspaper. She has bright red hair and sharp green eyes. Her skin is as pale as you would expect for a natural redhead with freckles to match.

“Hey, Mildred,” Lindsey says as she takes her seat on one of the bar stools at the serving counter.

Mildred watches over her thick glasses as Lindsey crosses her long thin legs. The short skirt Lindsey’s wearing doesn’t go unnoticed.

“Good morning, Lindsey,” Mildred answers. “Paul and Piper are in the back, and one of them should be out to take your order shortly. You should hope it’s Piper.”

“Hmm,” Lindsey replied. “Why is that?”

Mildred pretends to tilt a bottle back as if drinking from it. “Paul’s drunk. Again.”

Just then, Paul walks out through the kitchen door. “I’m not drunk,” Paul says in an exasperated tone. “And you know I can hear you, right, Mildred?”

“I know you can hear me, and I wouldn’t say anything that I wouldn’t say to your face.” Mildred looks up at Lindsey and says, “Paul’s drunk.”

Paul exhales deeply. Deciding to let it go, Paul greets Lindsey. “Good morning, Lindsey. Coffee with hazelnut creamer and sugar?”

“You know me so well,” Lindsey answers with a smile.

Paul brings over the hazelnut creamer and sugar and then fills Lindsey’s coffee cup. When he walks back to the kitchen, Lindsey attempts to get Mildred’s attention.

"Psst," Lindsey tries to whisper. "Psst," she tries again a little louder. Mildred looks up at her. "Someone got a DUI last night," she mouths, pointing at the kitchen.

"A DUI?" Mildred almost screams just to be sure Paul heard her. "I knew he was drunk."

Lindsey calls the jail every morning before she leaves the house to see if anything exciting happened that she would need to hurry up and write about before the day's paper gets printed. Paul's DUI was not important enough that it can't wait until the following day. But she didn't think it wouldn't hurt to give Mildred something to talk about a day early.

Piper walks out of the kitchen with another tray of freshly made bear claws. She places them in the glass case while Paul cleans up the kitchen.

"Hi, Lindsey."

"Hey, Piper."

"Anything exciting happen throughout the night?"

Mildred looks over her glasses at Lindsey.

"Nothing to speak of."

"That's good."

"Good for who?" Lindsey asks, almost irked by Piper's reply.

"The people who live here," Piper answers, almost shocked at Lindsey's question.

"I'm a reporter. That's how I make my money. It would be nice to have a good story to write about every now and then."

“Write about the 4-H program at the middle school.”

Lindsey rolls her eyes and crosses her other leg. “I need something a little more interesting than pigs and cows.”

“You could always move to a bigger city,” Paul offers as he takes the tray from his mother.

“You’d like that, wouldn’t you, Paul?” Paul thinks to himself that he’d like that just fine. “Then who would inform the good people of this community that once again you can’t control your drinking?”

Paul glares at Lindsey before walking back into the kitchen. Piper wipes down the already clean counter as she tries to stay out of it.

After Mildred finishes her doughnut, she begins to yell for Paul.

“Paul. Hey, Paul. I know you can hear me. Could you bring me another doughnut?”

It’s unusual for Mildred to have two doughnuts so early in the morning.

“I can get it for you, Mildred,” Piper says.

“Let me have a little fun with the boy, Piper.”

Piper isn’t sure what Mildred has planned for her son, but she is interested to see what it is. She knows Mildred won’t be as easy on her son as she has been with the driving under the influence charges.

Mildred yells again, “Hey, Paul.”

“Yes, Mildred. I can hear you.” Paul places the last tray of cinnamon rolls in the showcase and grabs Mildred another glazed doughnut.

"On your way over here, Paul, can I get you to walk on that straight line?" Mildred asks as she points to one of the lines that separate the square tiles on the floor.

Mildred and Lindsey both bust out in laughter. Piper tries hard to not join in on the fun. Paul tries to show off and hopscotches on the tile floor but stumbles as he takes the doughnut over to Mildred. Piper knows it's all done in fun, but she's still upset with her son for not making better decisions.

The morning rush begins to fill up the place and Mildred waits until it is good and packed before making her next joke about Paul's DUI. As he begins to start another pot of coffee, Mildred yells, "There you go again, operating machinery under the influence. I should make a citizen's arrest."

Paul pushes the start button on the coffee pot and heads back to the kitchen.

"Mom, do you think she's going to keep making jokes all morning?"

"I'm sure of it. You know how she is. You'll be lucky if it doesn't last the week."

"Why must she embarrass me like that?" Paul looks at his mother and then he says, "It's my payback for embarrassing my family, isn't it?" Piper looks at her son. She loves him, but he also embarrasses her at times like this. But she would never tell him that. Instead of saying anything, she just remains quiet. "Do you think Hannah can help me?" he asks.

Hannah is Piper's oldest child. She's a secretary at the Clerk of Courts, and Paul thinks because he has an inside connection she can get him out of trouble whenever she wants. Judges don't usually take too kindly to family interference. When the courts give you a break, you should avoid making the same mistake again at any cost.

"You mean like she did the last time?" There's no denying the tone in her voice. Piper is tired of her son's lack of responsibility and she knows this kind of thing also puts added stress on her daughter.

"I know it's a mess and I promise I'll straighten up."

This isn't the first time Paul's said these exact words. "You can ask her and see what she says."

"Me?"

"That's right. You want her help, you ask her for it."

"I thought you could."

"I know you did. I helped you the last time and you turned around and did the exact same thing. I'm sorry, but this time you're on your own, Paul."

Paul wants to be mad at his mother but deep down he knows she is right. This might be a hard lesson to learn. If his mother feels this way, he is sure Hannah will, too.

The bell over the door jingles as the door is pulled open. The entire room grows quiet as the patrons watch Ethel walk into the room. She's pulling her metal shopping cart behind her.

"Sounds like Ethel just walked in," Piper says to Paul inside the kitchen. "I better head out and try to keep the peace. Can you finish cleaning up in here?"

"Gladly, as long as I don't have to go back out there and hear Mildred anymore. Do you want me to grab your referee jersey and whistle?" Paul jokes.

"Keep it on standby," Piper says as she walks out of the room.

Ethel Bowers is the town's old maid. She can't get along with anyone and it's no wonder that she's never been married and has remained childless. It's been a few decades since anyone in town has known her to have a male friend. At her present age, she probably just gave up on ever meeting anyone. Ethel is about the same age as Mildred. They disagree as much as any husband and wife, maybe more. If one says something, the other disagrees just for the sake of disagreeing. They couldn't agree on the color of the sky. That seems to be the way Ethel is with all of the townspeople. There's something about that woman that aggravates others.

Every morning, Ethel comes into the shop with a thermos and a frown. She drinks the shop's coffee while she's there and then fills her thermos with the free coffee before she leaves. She doesn't just do it at the coffeehouse; she also takes advantage of the free coffee at the beauty salon, the library, and the local market. Anyplace that offers free coffee, she takes full advantage of it just like Mildred does.

It isn't fifteen minutes after Ethel arrives that half of the customers have left, including Lindsey, and Ethel's in her first argument. She chooses to give the butcher a hard time because she got sick a couple weeks ago and swore he either poisoned her or he and his wife are selling bad meat at their market.

The market is owned and operated by fifty-year-old Bob Stevens and his wife, Barb. His family has owned the butcher shop and market for as long as Mildred can remember. He and his wife are the owners and operators of the establishment.

"Are you sure you didn't come down with the flu?" Barb asks.

"Don't you think I know the difference between the flu and food poisoning?"

The last thing a butcher needs is someone accusing him of poisoning the food or selling bad meat. Lucky for Bob and Barb, most everyone in town knows how Ethel is. She's overly dramatic and a menace to the town and its residents.

After a few minutes of bickering with Ethel, Bob and Barb leave. That's when Mildred decides to chime in.

"Why don't you just tick off the man who plays with knives all day, Ethel?"

"I don't care if he plays with swords and pitchforks all day," Ethel snaps back. "He shouldn't be selling bad meat. And I bet I'm not the only person in town with food poisoning."

"The whole town buys meat from Bob and his wife yet you're the only one who got sick. You ever think that it may have been something else?"

"Yeah, I thought it could have been something else. Poison. That's what else it could have been."

"Nobody poisoned you. Though the whole town probably wishes someone would have."

Piper and Paul sit back and watch as the two argue back and forth. They're thankful that now the coffeehouse is mostly empty and no one is here to witness the bickering.

"Well, the whole town can just keep wishing. I haven't been around this long by accident. Besides, Doc Simms just gave me a clean bill of health. Looks like I'll be around for many more years to come."

Mildred blows out a puff of air. This is not news she wants to hear so early in the day: Her nemesis could outlive her and possibly others in Pineapple Grove. Mildred is hoping to have some peace in her life without being taunted by Ethel. Piper is also secretly wishing for peace in her coffeehouse. Paul is just wishing Ethel and Mildred would both fall off the earth and float away into deep space while Lindsey would be thrilled if someone was poisoned in the small town. It would be the break she's looking for.

Ethel looks up at Piper. "I heard that boy of yours got into some trouble last night."

Piper glares over at Mildred, who she suspects is the culprit for spreading the unwanted news.

"And who did you hear that from?"

"Heard it on the street on my way over here this morning."

Piper looks out the window and although it's early, the streets are already coming alive. How is it possible for others to already know about Paul? It's a small town. Just as Mildred and Lindsey already knew, Piper was sure others would also know. Lindsey has a big mouth, which might be what makes her a great reporter.

"It's being taken care of."

"Is your daughter helping him out with this charge, too?"

Piper blows out a puff of air. "Do you want a doughnut or some coffee to go, perhaps?"

Ethel must have decided that would be enough for one day. "Coffee to go would be nice."

Normally, Piper would fill a to-go cup for the customer, but she knows Ethel wants her thermos filled to the brim. She wonders whether Ethel actually drinks all the coffee she takes, but Piper's just glad Ethel's leaving.

~~~

Ethel leaves Bean There, Dunk That and heads to Sally's Salon to get her hair done. She's early for her appointment, but she doesn't care. It'll give her time to gossip with the others.

When she walks into the salon, she signs in and takes a seat on one of the black metal chairs lining the windows. She opens her thermos and pours herself a cup of the steaming hot brew. She would never let Piper know that she had the best coffee in town. A compliment like that could ruin Ethel's reputation, a reputation that took her years to build. She knew it wasn't a good reputation but it was hers and she was proud of it. She had proudly out-nastied the competition.

Ethel watches as Lindsey pays her bill. "You still working for the newspaper?" Ethel asks Lindsey sweetly.

Lindsey knows Ethel is anything but sweet. "I am, why?"

"Just asking."

Lindsey flips her newly styled hair and takes a seat beside Ethel. She crosses her long thin legs. "Why are you asking, Ethel?"

"By the length of your skirt and the amount of cleavage you're showing, I bet someone might suggest you have a nighttime job." Ethel sips her coffee. "If you know what I mean."

Lindsey knows exactly what she means. "Now, Ethel," Lindsey says, inhaling deeply and pushing her well-endowed breasts out even further. "You wouldn't be starting rumors about me now, would you?"
~~~

"It's not me, Lindsey. But I did just come from Piper's place and a few people were talking over there."

Lindsey looks shocked. "About me?"

"I'm not saying as I don't want to be in the middle of something."

Lindsey isn't sure whether to believe Ethel or not. When has Ethel never wanted to be in the midst of a rumor. After all, the rumor mill is a term Lindsey was sure made necessary because of Ethel. Lindsey stands and flips her hair again. She wiggles her hips and pulls down on her tight, black mini skirt.

"How are you feeling, Ethel?" Lindsey asks, not really caring how Ethel feels. "I heard you were nearly poisoned to death by Butcher Bob last week."

So, it was poisoning? I knew it, Ethel thinks to herself. "Much better. Thank you." Ethel holds out her nearly empty cup/lid to her thermos. "Would you be a dear and refill my coffee for me?"

"It's my pleasure." Lindsey takes her cup and refills it for her from the free coffee station in the salon, before strutting out the door.

Ethel drinks her coffee as she waits to be called back for her hair appointment. She's a little disappointed when there's no gossip to listen to or partake in.

Remembering what she regarded as her near death from the poisoned meat she got from Butcher Bob, Ethel begins to feel ill. She goes into the restroom until the nausea passes.

When Ethel returns from the restroom, Sally cuts and styles Ethel's hair in an uncomfortable silence. It's not like Ethel to be quiet for so long.

"Are you feeling okay, Ethel?" Sally asks.

"Why? Have you heard something about the poisoned meat Butcher Bob sold me?"

"No, I haven't heard anything. Well, nothing that hasn't come from you, that is."

Ethel places her hand on her upset stomach. "Something needs to be done about Butcher Bob and his tainted meat. Mark my words, I bet someone's gonna die one of these days and it's gonna be all his fault."

"Well, I hope not," Sally says. "He's the only butcher and market in town."

Sally shops at the local market quite often and she's known Bob and Barb to sell only the freshest meat available. Bob is a butcher, after all.

When Sally's done with Ethel's hair, Ethel picks at it while looking at herself in the mirror. The look on her face is more of a grimace than a smile. But of course, Ethel has only one look and this is it. Without saying a word, Ethel walks over, pays her bill, and fills her thermos with coffee just before she turns to leave.

"Should I put you down for your next appointment?" Sally asks, picking up the pen to write in the appointment book.

Ethel places her thermos into her cart with wheels and opens the door before saying, "I won't be back until you get someone in here who knows what they're doing." Then she walks out the door and leaves.

Sally's mouth falls open. She's known Ethel to be rude to others, but she's never witnessed it firsthand. She throws the hairbrush at the now closed door and yells, "I wish Butcher Bob would poison you."

~~~

Lindsey storms into the Bean There, Dunk That with an attitude. Lucky for Piper, the coffeehouse is near closing. Lindsey doesn't like anyone accusing her of being slutty, even if it might be the truth. The only person in the coffeehouse is Mildred, who is still sitting in the exact same spot as when Lindsey left hours earlier. Lindsey wonders if she is back for more coffee and doughnuts or is she still here from earlier? Mildred smiles as she continues her crocheting.

"Hey, Lindsey. Did you forget something?" Piper asks as she wipes off the counter.

"No, I just left Sally's…" she begins to say.

"I can tell. Your hair looks great. I love the cut on you. It's very flattering."

"Thank you." Lindsey smiles and touches her hair as she scans the room for a mirror.

"Do you want some coffee? I might also have a few glazed doughnuts left I can offer you."

Lindsey remembers why she's here and it's not for coffee or doughnuts. "Ethel just told me someone here was suggesting to her and to others that I might have a night job."

Piper stops wiping off the counter. "You're still at the newspaper, right?"

Lindsey straightens her skirt with a little hip action. "Of course, I am."

Mildred pushes her glasses down further on her nose and looks up and down at Lindsey. But she remains quiet.

"That's sort of a night job, isn't it?" Piper asks.
~~~

“Not that kind of job,” Lindsey says with irritation in her voice.

“Oh,” Piper says when she realizes the other meaning of “night job.”

Mildred looks away and tends to her crocheting. “Do you have a second job, Lindsey?”

“No.”

“Then why let that old goat get under your skin?”

“Because… it’s just hurtful.” Then Lindsey remembers how Ethel is with everyone. She walks closer to Piper. “You didn’t suggest that, did you?”

“It never even crossed my mind. And no one else said anything of the kind either. At least not when I was around.”

“Ugh!” Lindsey screams before storming out of the coffeehouse. “I swear I hate that old ninny.”

“She isn’t the only one,” whispers Mildred.

~~~

Paul finishes closing the back of the coffeehouse and then walks to the police station to see about getting his car out of impound. He still needs to talk to his sister, but he wouldn’t do that while she’s at work. He isn’t sure what she’ll have to say and he’s pretty sure it will be something he doesn’t want others to hear. Walking the few miles in the heat to the police station also gives him time to think about his mistakes. He knows one thing; he doesn’t like walking, even if it is good for you.

Piper closes up the front of the coffeehouse while Mildred stays and crochets her afghan. Piper isn’t sure why Mildred stays in the shop from open to close. It has never bothered
~~~

Piper to have her here. Mildred is a gossiper, but her gossip is usually harmless.

"Mildred, I have two glazed doughnuts and some coffee left. Do you want to take them home with you?"

"You're closing already?" Mildred looks over her glasses at the now empty coffeehouse.

"I am. It's two o'clock." Piper thinks it would be nice to not have to worry about the time of day. Just do as you please whenever you want to. "You don't have to go home, but you can't stay here," Piper says in a teasing tone.

Mildred stands as she pulls her floral dress out of her butt cheeks. before picking up her crocheting bag. One of her stockings has now fallen down to her ankle while the other one is where it should be; above her knee. Piper notices that her black shoes are worn as Mildred walks on the sides of her feet. Piper's never noticed that before about Mildred.

"Have you ever known me to refuse anything that was free?"

"No. I can't say I have."

"And you won't either."

Piper gets the doughnuts packaged up and watches as Mildred places the bag carefully in her crochet bag. Piper also refills her extra-large insulated cup with the leftover coffee. Mildred struggles with her bag before opening the shop's door.

"Maybe you should get one of those rolling carts like Ethel has?" Piper suggests.

"No. No. I can manage just fine. I'm not that old yet."

Piper doesn't know for sure, but she believes Mildred and Ethel are about the same age.

"Are you heading home, Mildred?"

"Nope, it's too early for that. I'm heading to the library to return some books. Then I'll go over to the market to refill my coffee. For dinner, I'm thinking of having something over at Banks' pub, then I might stay for a toddy or two before turning in for the night." She readjusts her bag while holding the large insulated cup. "You should stop over there one day. The owner's pretty easy on the eyes."

"Toddy? As in an alcoholic beverage?" Mildred still drinks at her age? This is news to Piper.

"Yes, that's right. A little midday gin and tonic never hurt anyone."

Piper thinks about her son and his obsessive drinking. She couldn't agree with Mildred's statement.

"What pub are you going to?"

"There's a new one along the river that just recently opened. It's called River Banks or Banks' Pub or something of that nature."

"I'll have to try it out."

"You should. They have great food and the drinks ain't bad either."

"Have fun and be careful. I'd hate for something to happen to you on your way home."

Mildred waves a hand and leaves without another word.

Piper locks up and heads home. When she opens the front door, Bailey's standing there wagging her tail and barking with excitement.

"Hey, girl. You miss Momma?"

Bailey barks, letting her know she missed her and that she needs to go outside now. Piper sets down her bag, purse, and keys, before getting Bailey's leash to go outside.

Piper walks her around the neighborhood since Bailey's been confined to the house for longer than usual. She sees Ethel walking down the street but doesn't say anything to her. Ethel is in one of her moods, which it makes it nearly impossible to be near her because she's so unpleasant. In fact, Piper tries to avoid Ethel and walks in the other direction.

Once home, Piper showers and goes to the local market to get something for dinner. She knows her daughter, Hannah, will be here as soon as she gets off work. She will have seen her brother's name on the court docket for tomorrow and will be furious at his carelessness and lack of respect for her. She works for the clerk of courts, so does she really want to be humiliated by her drunken brother, again? Everyone in the office and in the building will know her brother was arrested, again.

When Piper walks into the market, she sees Ethel at the self-serve coffee station filling her thermos with the free coffee Bob and Barb set out for their paying customers. Ethel had just accused Butcher Bob of trying to poison her, so why would she be inside his store? Obviously, for the free coffee. Ethel said the meat was poisoned, but she didn't mention anything about the coffee. Without saying a word, Ethel places the thermos in her rolling cart and buys a loaf of bread before leaving.

People from larger cities often question why and how we can afford to offer free coffee in Pineapple Grove. I'm not sure it's free in every establishment. I know at the coffeehouse we offer free refills. Paul and I set up the self-serve coffee station to make it easier on us. The customers can help themselves to refills while Paul and I attend to other things. If someone comes in and helps himself or herself to a free coffee without making a purchase, I probably wouldn't say anything. Places like the market and the beauty salon offer it to their guests for free. If the customers like the coffee well enough in the market, hopefully they'll purchase it off the shelf. In the beauty salon, it's just good business to offer your patrons something to drink while they wait. I'm sure some people would like to see a free beer and wine station set up in one of the many establishments here in Pineapple Grove. I might be one of those people. I'm sure Paul and Scott would be another.

I've heard from the old timers, and I believe it to be true, that it's a small-town tradition for businesses to offer free coffee. Who am I to argue with tradition?

It's also been said that when Ethel's and Mildred's coffee cools and they think no one's looking, they water the plants with it. That's easy enough to believe since they're the ones who partake the most.

"If she never comes back in here again, it'll be too soon," Bob says as he wipes his hands off with the white kitchen towel. He's behind the meat counter wearing a white apron while his wife is at the register.

Neither Piper nor Barb replies. Both understand his frustration with Ethel.

Thinking about what to have for dinner, Piper decides on an easy dish of spaghetti and meatballs. She already has the pasta and some homemade sauce in the freezer at home, so she purchases Italian sausage and fresh ground beef for the meatballs.

"How is everything, Bob?" Piper asks when she places her order at the meat counter. She looks around the store and it seems busy, which is a good thing considering the things Ethel has been saying about being poisoned.

“Busy. Thankfully the wacky broad’s accusations didn’t harm my business.”

“That’s good.”

“Can you imagine if everyone in town believed her? We’d be out of business.”

Bob doesn’t wait for her to answer as he opens the slider door to the cooler to retrieve the meat she ordered. Piper is thankful that Ethel’s rumors of being poisoned are just that. Rumors. She’d hate to travel further than she has to for her groceries. When Bob hands Piper her purchase, she thanks him before going to the register to pay for it.

“How are you, Barb?”

Barb readjusts her bobby pin in her hair. “I’m fine, but Bob has some unwanted stress.”

“I noticed. He seems more stressed than usual. Is it because of Ethel?”

“It is. We went over to the inn to visit with Stephanie earlier today and Ethel was there filling her thermos with coffee.”

The inn is on the west side of town. Piper’s surprised Ethel is able to walk that far. Why would she go so far out of her way when every small business owner in town offers free coffee to their patrons?

“When Ethel saw us walk in, she started accusing Bob of poisoning her,” Barb continues.

“Yikes. I hope no one else was there to hear her.”

"A few guests were still lingering and you know they got an earful."

"I'm sorry. Is Ethel like this because she's old and becoming senile?" Piper pays cash for her purchase.

"I don't know what it is, but the rumors could kill our business and Bob's reputation."

"You're right, it could. I hope this ends soon for you both."

"The only way it'll end is when Ethel's no longer around to keep things stirred up."

Piper says her goodbyes and heads home to start dinner.

~~~

Just as dinner's about done, Hannah bursts through the front door. "Where's that loser son of *yours*?"

"*Your* brother's upstairs getting ready for dinner."

"Did you know he was in jail again the other night?" Piper remains quiet. "Of course you did. You're the one who bonded him out." Hannah takes a seat at the barstool. "What's his excuse this time? 'I wasn't drunk' or 'I was framed' or was it 'Someone roofied my drink'?"

Paul walks into the room freshly showered. "Hey, that's a good one. I never thought of that. Maybe my defense should be Butcher Bob roofied my drink."

Piper rolls her eyes because she's pretty sure Bob didn't poison anyone and her mother's intuition tells her this is going to lead to a huge fight between her adult children.

"You wouldn't!" Hannah says.

"Nah, but it would be a great defense. If I didn't like the old man butcher as much as I do, I might."
~~~

Piper drains the water from the pasta.

Hannah glares over at her brother and says sarcastically, "I think it's funny you're getting ready to do six months for your second D.U.I. in a year, and you're able to joke about it."

Paul sits at the dining room table and kicks his feet up on a chair opposite him. He interlocks his fingers behind his head. "I have a sister with connections."

"You think I'm going to help you get out of this again?" She doesn't wait for Paul to answer. "I wouldn't bet on it."

Paul looks concerned as he sits up straighter in the chair. "Why not?"

"Because you don't learn. You're irresponsible. And you take people for granted." Hannah leans back on the barstool. "I'm not the one who messed up, Paul. You messed up, now you need to own it. Maybe some jail time is just what you need to finally grow up."

Paul goes upstairs and sulks while Piper and Hannah enjoy a quiet dinner together.

After dinner, Piper's glad to see Hannah and Paul are outside talking while Bailey runs loose in the fenced-in backyard. She doesn't know if Hannah can help her brother, but she knows Hannah loves him and will help if she can.

~~~

The next morning, Paul and Piper drive to work together since Paul's car's still in impound. He can't get it out until after his first court hearing. He knows the hard work involved in opening the coffee and doughnut shop so he's agreed to help his mother before going to court this morning. Last night after Paul talked more calmly to his
~~~

sister about his charges, she didn't say she would help him but she also didn't say she wouldn't.

As soon as the last tray of cinnamon rolls comes out of the oven, Paul unlocks the front door and helps Mildred into the shop. He doesn't know if her arrival is perfect timing or if she waited in one on the rockers on the front porch in the dark for the coffeehouse to open.

Once again, he takes her crocheting bag and wonders what is in it to make it so heavy. She follows behind him as he leads the way to her favorite table. While Piper stocks the glass display case with the doughnuts and cinnamon rolls, Paul takes Mildred's order of one coffee with cream and sugar and one glazed doughnut easy on the glaze — as if he can control that once it's made.

"How are you, Mildred?" Piper calls over the counter.

"I'm not doing too good this morning."

"Oh, I'm sorry to hear that." Piper watches her with concern.

"My legs got the cramps last night so I couldn't sleep."

"Oh, I'm sorry." Mildred walked here so her leg cramps must be better. "Are you a diabetic?"

"No, not me. Doc Simms said I needed to drink more water, and he said a banana every now and then wouldn't hurt."

"I see. Are you drinking more water?"

"I'm drinking more coffee, does that count?" Piper doesn't answer. "Then this mornin' my bowels didn't move so I had to take something for that." Piper looks over at Paul as she's at a loss for words. Paul shrugged his shoulders. He wasn't touching that comment. "Finally, the bowels moved and then my bunions started hurtin'. Took me forever to find some shoes that fit."

Piper avoids looking down at Mildred's feet. She isn't sure she could stomach what she might see. Mildred might be wearing open-toe shoes that reveal her bunions.

Lindsey comes into the coffeehouse next. Piper's thankful for the distraction. Lindsey smiles politely at Mildred as she makes her way to the counter. Paul brings her a coffee with hazelnut creamer and one sugar.

"Anything new happen last night?" Paul asks the newspaper reporter.

"No. Nothing." Lindsey pouts. "I'd almost kill for a big story."

Paul laughs. "Be careful what you wish for. It's a small town and you know how gossip and rumors spread." Paul looks over at Mildred.

Mildred clears her throat. "You wouldn't be talking about me now, would you, Paul?"

"No, Mildred. Just making a statement."

"Hmm," Mildred says, crocheting her afghan. "You must have stayed in last night, Paul."

"Why would you say that?"

"You don't smell of alcohol this mornin'."

Even to Piper, this statement is funny. Lindsey and Piper both try to disguise their chuckle.

"Ha-ha. Very funny, Mildred."

Paul heads to the kitchen to clean up and leaves his mom to the customers. She's much better at customer service than he is. As soon as the kitchen's clean, Paul tells the patrons goodbye, kisses his mother on the cheek, and leaves out the back door for his court appearance.

After a few seconds, he rushes back inside. The look on his face scares Piper.

"What is it?" Piper asks.

"It's Ethel."

"What's that old hag done now?" Mildred scoffs.

"She's in the alley. She's fallen and I think she's unconscious."

"What?" Piper shouts. "When? Where?"

"Now! Outside. She's behind the coffeehouse."

Everyone stands and races out the back door.

Ethel is lying in the alley behind the coffeehouse.

Paul does a double take — it looks like Lindsey's smiling. Mildred, who has hobbled outside with the others, also notices the smile.

Piper and Lindsey rush over to Ethel, who's lying face down, her cart on wheels tipped over.

Piper checks Ethel for a pulse. There's no denying it. Ethel's dead.

CHAPTER 2

Mildred finally makes her way out the back door shortly after everyone else. She sees Lindsey pulling out her cell phone.

“Good idea, call Sheriff Abbott,” Piper says.

“I’m not calling the sheriff, I’m calling Hunter, my photographer. Paul, you call the sheriff.”

Mildred squeezes her way between Piper and Lindsey to get a better look at Ethel’s body.

“I can’t find a pulse,” Piper cries.

“You still wanna make that comment about killing someone to get a good story?” Mildred asks Lindsey.

“That was just a saying. I didn’t mean it literally.”

“I wonder what happened?” Piper asks, not seeing any obvious cause of injury, but also not wanting to move the body to look for any.

“Maybe she was hit by a drunk driver,” Mildred says as she looks at the back door of the coffeehouse that Paul just walked through to call the police.

“Paul’s DUI was yesterday, Mildred,” Piper says, defending her son. “Now’s not the time Mildred.”

“I wasn’t implying that it was Paul,” Mildred says. “He isn’t the only person in this town who has ever been charged with drinking and driving.”

Piper knows Mildred was talking about Paul regardless of what she’s saying now.

Mildred will probably accuse everyone in the town before all is said and done.

Paul comes back, still on the phone with the 911 operator.

“Yes, I’m sure she’s not breathing,” he says into the phone. “Okay, just try to hurry.” Paul hangs up the phone then looks at his watch. “They’re on their way, but I gotta go to the courthouse. They’ll issue a bench warrant for my arrest if I’m not there.”

“I understand. Go on, Paul. We got this.”

Paul leaves without looking back.

Moments later, the sounds of sirens are heard in the distance. Surprisingly, Lindsey’s photographer, Hunter Gallagher, is on the scene first. Piper wonders if Hunter doesn’t work part-time as a racecar driver since he got here so fast. Hunter’s wearing a bright yellow shirt. It’s not fluorescent, but Piper’s first thought is that it could possibly glow in the dark. She doesn’t know Hunter but wonders if this is his normal clothing attire. The sheriff follows closely behind with the ambulance.

After the sheriff tapes off the scene, he takes photos of the body before the medics take over. Sheriff Alexander Abbott gets everyone back inside the coffeehouse to question them. Piper offers him a coffee and a doughnut that he gladly accepts. In fact, he accepts several doughnuts.

“Who’s going to tell me what happened?” the sheriff begins, taking a sip of his coffee.

“We were all in here. Well, me, Lindsey, Mildred, and Paul,” Piper begins. “Paul finished cleaning up in the kitchen and was leaving out the back door to head to the courthouse. Seconds later, he ran back in with the look of fear on his face. He told us what he saw and we all ran out back to see.”

"Where's Paul now?" Sheriff Abbott asks.

"Well, after he called 911 he left for the courthouse. He has a court hearing this morning."

"That'll be postponed. They kind of need me there to hold the hearing. So, you're saying Paul left the scene?"

Piper looks shocked. "The scene of what?"

"Until this is ruled as an accidental death, this is considered a crime scene."

"She's nearly eighty years old. You can't possibly think her death wasn't from natural causes. Who would murder Ethel?"

As soon as the words leave Piper's mouth, she already knows the answer. Half the people in Pineapple Grove disliked Ethel, but did they want her dead? Ethel certainly thought Butcher Bob did.

"You might be surprised." Sheriff Abbott looks over at Lindsey and her photographer. "What about you, Mr. Gallagher? When did you get here?"

"Lindsey called me after they found Ethel and told me what happened. It just so happened I was heading here anyway and was only a couple blocks away when she called."

"Your first thought was to call your photographer, Ms. Miles?" The sheriff raises a brow.

"Yeah. I wasn't the only one here who could have called y'all. After all, I am a reporter." Lindsey straightens her short skirt.

"Let me see if I got this right. Paul found the body out back and then leaves after he calls 911. Lindsey calls her photographer instead of calling 911. The photographer makes it on the scene before I do. Did anyone else see or hear anything that may have looked or sounded suspicious?"

"If you ask me, it all kind of looks and sounds suspicious," Mildred says.

"Yeah, but anything in particular?"

No one answers. Sheriff Abbott finishes his questioning and his fifth doughnut then heads out back to his squad car. Before he is able to pull away, Mildred walks out from around the building as quickly as her wobbly legs will carry her.

"Sheriff Abbott," she yells, waving one hand over her head.

He gets out of the police car. "What is it, Mildred?"

"I didn't wanna say anything in there in front of everyone, but I thought you should know."

"Know what?"

"Well, right before Paul found Ethel, Lindsey made the comment that she would kill for a good story. I just thought it looked funny that she would say that shortly after she got here, and then a body turns up. Then when she called Hunter and he just happened to be right around the corner. I don't know, Sheriff. It doesn't sound right if you ask me."

"Thank you, Mildred. I'll make sure to add that to my notes."

While Sheriff Abbott jots her statement into his notepad, Mildred leaves. He checks the alley one last time for clues. When he sees Ethel's cart leaning against Piper's coffeehouse, he walks over to it and looks through it before removing an item. Then he opens the back door to the coffeehouse.

"Piper," he calls out.

"Yeah. What is it?" she asks, walking through the kitchen door.

"I would take this with me, but the car's loaded down with boxes I need to take to archives. Can I store this in here for a while?"

"Sure. Don't you need it for evidence?" Piper asks, partly joking.

"I took what I thought might be useful in the investigation."

"Oh. This really is a murder investigation?" Piper wasn't sure how she felt about that.

"Until her cause of death is confirmed, it's considered suspicious. I'll call you later or I'll send one of my guys over to collect it."

"No hurry. It's fine here."

Word of Ethel's death spreads quickly around the small town. Bean There, Dunk That has a line of people waiting outside to get in and see what they can hear about the death. Rumors are already beginning to spread, and Butcher Bob seems to be the hottest topic of conversation. Maybe he did poison Ethel.

This could actually be good for business, Piper thinks to herself. The coffeehouse usually does well every day until Ethel comes in and chases most of the customers away. If Piper could only get Mildred to leave the shop today so the two-top table could actually get used for two people, business would be better. Better business means better revenue.

Piper walks over to Mildred. "Mildred, will there be anything else for you today?" Piper asks sweetly.

"I could use a little more coffee." Piper looks down at the still full cup. Mildred begins crocheting again. When Piper doesn't leave, Mildred looks back at her, then down at her full cup of coffee. "Thank you, dear. That'll be all for now."

Piper decides not to push the issue. Today shouldn't be any different from any other day. Surely Mildred won't be leaving while all this gossip is going on.

Paul returns shortly after saying that his court date was postponed. Piper is thrilled to see him since she needs to make another batch of glazed doughnuts.

Lindsey is in full conversation with her hairdresser, Sally, when Piper brings them their bill.

"Do you think she was murdered?" Sally asks.

"It doesn't matter what I think," Lindsey answers. "It's what the people of Pineapple Grove want to read about."

Sally says, "I just think everyone might be jumping to conclusions. The old hag might have just had a heart attack, and here everyone is trying to solve a murder and pointing the finger at the next person. I learned a long time ago that you shouldn't point your finger. Because when you have one finger pointing at someone else, you have *three fingers pointing right back at you*."

Piper agrees but remains silent.

Two o'clock comes and it's time to close the coffeehouse, but nobody seems to want to leave anytime soon. Piper has a photo shoot scheduled for three. She loves coffee and doughnuts, but Piper's second love is photography. She only does it professionally in her spare time and it's never enough.

Paul offers to stay to close up while Piper leaves out the back door where Ethel's body had been found only a few hours earlier. She shivers as she remembers the earlier scene. Ethel's lifeless body and her overturned cart. Hopefully the coroner will rule this as a death by natural causes soon and the townspeople can move on to less interesting gossip.

Piper drives to a private place along the water for the photo shoot. She's doing senior pictures for some of the high school girls. It's fun and relaxing. Piper wishes she had more time for this hobby. The girls are very photogenic and they laugh a lot, which causes Piper to also laugh. She realizes the news of Ethel's death doesn't affect everyone in Pineapple Grove. *Oh, to be young again,* Piper thinks to herself.

Piper heads home and edits the digital images before emailing them to Polly's Print Shop. The girls are in a hurry and Piper is happy to oblige. When she's done with that, Piper spends the rest of the evening wondering how Ethel had died. Did someone really dislike her enough to kill her? Who would do that? How would they do it? Ethel was found in back of the alley of the coffeehouse. There wasn't any blood. Piper was working, and she didn't hear a confrontation with anyone. Was it premeditated or spontaneous? Time and the Sheriff will tell.

~~~

The following morning Piper and Paul go to the coffeehouse together.

They're both shocked to see someone threw eggs on the building. The windows are now covered with dried egg yolk. Piper's thankful that no one spray-painted anything on the brick building. The egg is enough.
~~~

Piper nearly cries but Paul steps up and says, "You go inside, I'll get the hose to clean this up before we open."

Piper searches the dark street. "What if they're still here waiting for us?"

"This was done hours ago. It's already dried. Go on in, I'll be okay."

Piper stands there with her son looking at the mess. If he didn't clean it up, they would be forced to close the shop today. Piper decides she needs to call the sheriff to let him know. Maybe he can have someone patrol the area for a while. When she opens the door to the coffeehouse, there's a note on the floor that's been slid under the door. Piper shows Paul the note. "MURDERER" is written in a red marker.

"We should call the sheriff and report this."

"I'll call later."

When everything's ready, Paul unlocks the door and flips the "closed" sign over to "open". Like every morning, Mildred's the first to arrive.

"Looks like it rained only on your coffeehouse."

"Someone egged us," Paul says, not thinking about how fast those few words can travel around Pineapple Grove now that he's told Mildred.

"What! Who would do such a thing?"

"I don't know. But I hope it's the only time."

Paul takes her bag for her like he always does and leads her to her two-top table where she begins her crocheting. Paul takes her order and brings her a cup of coffee with cream and sugar. Moments later, Piper comes out of the kitchen with fresh doughnuts and takes a glazed one to Mildred.

At seven-thirty everyone in the coffeehouse is surprised when Mildred asks for her bill.

“Leaving us this early, Mildred?” Piper asks.

“Yes, I have some other things I have to tend to this morning. You shouldn’t sound so surprised. I do have a life outside of this place, you know.’’

Paul and Piper are surprised. They thought the coffeehouse was Mildred’s life.

“We never assumed you didn’t,” Piper lies. “We’ve just become accustomed to your company.”

“Well, it looks like you’ll just have to have someone else entertain you today,” Mildred says as she stuffs her crocheting into her bag, picks it up, and then heads out the door.

Paul leaves shortly after Mildred to go back to the courthouse for his postponed court hearing.

Just after 8:30, Paul watches as Mildred walks out of the courtroom he’s waiting to go into. Before he is about to enter the courtroom, a local lawyer who has been appointed to represent him walks over and advises him that his hearing has been postponed again. He wonders if Mildred’s appearance had something to do with his case.

“I walked all the way over here for nothing. You couldn’t call me to tell me that my court date was postponed?”

The attorney adjusts his tie. “I thought while you were here, we could see about getting your car out of impound.”

“Okay, let’s do this!

To Paul’s surprise, they released his car before he went to court. He’s sure his sister had something to do with that, but he won’t ask her. He arranges to have the car towed back to his mother's house. It'll have a boot on it so Paul can't drive it, but he's fine with that. The daily cost of storing his car at the impound lot is more than Paul wants to pay.

Paul leaves the courthouse and goes back to the shop to help his mother. Once they're alone in the kitchen, Paul tells Piper about Mildred being at the courthouse. It's not just women who gossip.

"It would be funny if Mildred had been arrested for a public intoxication charge." Paul laughs. "Or better yet, maybe public indecency." Piper gags at the thought of Mildred being indecent. Whatever Mildred's case was, Paul is already thinking of jokes he is planning on using in the presence of Mildred.

The morning carries on and the shop fills up and stays full until well after the two o'clock closing time. Just after closing, Piper gets a call from her daughter.

Piper picks up her cell phone. "Hello."

"Hey, Mom. What's up?"

"Just closing the shop."

"I spoke with the judge about Paul's DUI. To say the least, he's not pleased at all. He is willing to give him a break, but he wants you to be in his courtroom tomorrow morning at eight o'clock."

"He wants me in court tomorrow morning? I'm not charged with anything."

"I know that and so does he. He said he needs someone to help him out with something. He wouldn't say what it is. Believe me, I tried to find out. He said if you come tomorrow he'll hear Paul's case Monday morning and will give him a lighter sentence."

"Okay, I'll be there."

"I'll tell him."

"Hannah, thanks for talking to the judge about your brother."

"Don't tell him and this is my last time. He's on his own from now on."

Piper knows her daughter means it. She also knows Paul needs to grow up and take responsibility for his actions.

"I won't say anything."

She can't figure out why the judge would need to see her in court tomorrow. When Paul leaves for the day, she decides that since she personally knows Judge Liam Greer, she would just call him to find out what's going on herself. She was a bit bothered that he didn't call her himself.

After being placed on hold for several minutes, he finally answers the phone. "Judge Greer speaking."

"Liam, it's Piper."

"Hey, Piper," he says more cheerfully and less professionally.

"Hannah said you wanted to see me in the morning."

"I do. This can wait until morning."

"No, it can't. I don't like surprises."

Liam laughs. "I understand. I should have called you and asked you personally."

"Ask me what?"

"I need someone to be executor of Ethel Bowers' estate."

"Doesn't she have family?"

"She does, but no one well enough or young enough to handle the project."

"Executor of her estate? It sounds complex." *Piper wonders if the house Ethel lived in could be classified as an estate.*

"No, not at all."

"What will I need to do?"

"Does that mean you'll do it?"

"If there's no one else, I guess I'll have to."

"Thank you, I'll see you in the morning and we'll go over the details then."

"Fine. Hey, if you see the sheriff you might want to tell him to announce how Ethel died. Rumors are running crazy with people speculating that she was murdered."

"I heard him say as soon as he was certain of the cause of death he was going to announce it at a press conference."

Would a press conference be necessary if she died of natural causes? Piper suspects that Liam knows more than he's saying. She would have to wait like the others to find out the cause of death.

When she returns home, she sees Paul's car parked in the driveway with a boot on it. If people don't know about his DUI, they'll know once they see his car.

~~~

The following morning, Piper and Paul are disappointed to see the coffeehouse has been egged again. There's another note slid under the door with the word "MURDERER" hand written in red marker.
~~~

"I'll clean this up and later today we should buy a power washer to keep in the back."

"I'm sorry. Maybe we should sell the coffeehouse and move."

"We're not going to let anyone in Pineapple Grove force us away. When and if we decide to move, we'll do it on our own time."

It's the first time since Piper can remember that Mildred didn't come to the coffeehouse. She hopes Mildred's feeling okay.

Just before eight o'clock, Piper leaves Paul at the shop and heads to the courthouse. Outside of the courtroom door, Mildred's sitting on the wooden bench crocheting.

"Do you have court this morning, Mildred?" Piper asks.

"If you want to call it that. I don't know why these people keep bothering me. I just want to be left alone."

"May I ask what this has to do with?"

"It's Ethel. That rodent is still bothering me from the dead."

Before Piper can ask her to elaborate, the bailiff opens the doors and motions for Piper and Mildred to enter the room. After a couple short minutes, he yells for everyone to stand.

"All rise. Court is now in session. The Honorable Judge Liam Greer presiding."

Piper and Mildred stand as Judge Greer makes his way to the bench.

"You may be seated," he says as he takes his seat. Once everyone is seated he says, "The matter of the estate of Ethel Bowers is before the court this morning. Ethel has a last will and testament and in the will she appointed

Mildred Moore as the executor of her estate. Yesterday, this court was prepared to appoint Mildred as executor; however, Ms. Moore advised us that she did not wish to take part in any of Ms. Bowers' affairs. Is that still true today, Ms. Moore?"

Mildred stands and says, "That is correct, your honor. I don't know why *that* woman would appoint me anything of hers. We haven't gotten along since high school and as you can tell that was a very long time ago." Mildred sits down.

"The court is prepared to pick a replacement. Ms. Armstrong, could you please stand?" Piper stands. "Ms. Armstrong, as you can see, the court needs someone to act as executor for the estate of Ethel Bowers. It's not a complicated task. She has spelled out what she wishes to be done. I just need you to carry out those wishes. The estate will compensate you for your time with five percent of the total estate value. I will take it as a personal favor if you would agree to do this."

"I'm not exactly sure what to do, but I'm sure I can handle it."

"Thank you, Ms. Armstrong. Before you leave here this morning, meet me in my chambers so we can go over Ethel's wishes." Piper nods. "Therefore, this court appoints Ms. Piper Armstrong as executor of the estate of Ethel Bowers. Ms. Moore, you are hereby relieved from the duties. That will be all. Court is adjourned." Judge Greer slams his gavel and walks out of the courtroom.

Mildred walks out of the courtroom. The bailiff leads Piper to the judge's chambers and opens the door for her; she's surprised to find the judge already sitting at his overly large desk. He's no longer wearing the black robe he had on in the courtroom.

"Piper, I want to thank you for helping out on such short notice."

"You're welcome. I'm glad to help."

"I spoke with Hannah about Paul's DUI. Monday morning I'll sentence him to three days in jail with some community service. I hope you understand I can't just make this go away."

"I understand. It's time he grows up and learns a lesson."

"I feel the same way. I like the boy, but he's too old for this behavior to continue." Piper couldn't agree more, but she hopes that the judge doesn't lecture her on her son's bad behavior. "His service to the community will consist of helping you with the physical labors of this estate. Things may need to be moved out of the house. He can do all the heavy lifting. Do you have any questions?"

"What am I supposed to do with Ethel's things?"

"In her last will and testament, she mentions a sister. Ethel states in the will that what the sister doesn't want will be sold off and all the money given to her sister. Like I said, it's not a complicated task."

"I guess I'll start by taking inventory. Then should I list everything with an auctioneer?"

"Sounds like a good place to start. Here's the keys to her home, address, and her sister's name and phone number." He reaches in his desk drawer and hands Piper Ethel's house key and a piece of paper with the information. "You can start anytime you're ready."

"Can I ask someone to help me with the process?"

"Yes. Make sure it's someone you can trust. You never know what you'll find, and we don't need someone spreading more rumors than necessary." Piper has no idea what she will find, but she knows the speed of rumors in Pineapple Grove is as fast as the speed of sound and telephone connections. She takes the keys and a piece of paper with the information on it. "Here's the information of Ethel's sister and the address of Ethel's duplex. She lived in one side while the other side is vacant. You'll want to call the sister to see what all she wants in the house before selling or tossing anything."

"The sister had been notified of her sister's passing, right?"

"She has."

That's one job Piper doesn't want: to notify one sister of another sister's passing.

"And is the house available for me to enter?"

"I spoke with the sheriff this morning. They already searched it and took what they needed."

Piper wasn't sure what the sheriff would have taken or needed out of Ethel's house.

"Okay. I'll be in touch."

"Thank you, Piper."

Piper walks out of the room and down the hall to see Mildred sitting at the wooden bench crocheting. "Would you like a ride, Mildred?"

"That would be nice, if you don't mind."

Once inside the car Piper asks Mildred where she wants to be dropped off. Piper isn't surprised when Mildred says she is going to the coffeehouse.

They ride in silence. Piper wants to ask why Mildred thinks Ethel would have wanted her as executor of her estate, but she could sense that Mildred doesn't want to discuss it. When they arrive back at the shop, Piper sees that the place is packed again.

"Better hope we have a table for you," Piper says.

"If not, I'll wait in the rocker outside until one opens up. It's nice out and it'll give me a chance to think about what's happening."

Piper knows that Mildred and Ethel weren't close, but she senses a sadness in Mildred. Why would Mildred be sad over Ethel's death? They were nearly the same age. Maybe it's a reminder to Mildred that she won't live forever.

"I'll come get you when a table clears."

"Thank you, dear."

Piper greets the customers before walking into the kitchen to see Paul. She puts on her apron and heads back out to the dining area.

"What's going on?" Paul asks.

"I'll explain later."

"I'm glad you're back. It's been a mad house."

"Looks like you did a good job keeping everything running."

"I tried."

Piper looks at Paul and she sees the sincerity in his eyes.

"Thank you."

Piper walks out of the kitchen.

It shouldn't have been a surprise when Lindsey asks, "Did you take the job?"

"What job?" Piper asks.

"Over Ethel's estate. I know Ethel appointed Mildred and she refused to do it."

"How do you know this already when it just happened?"

"I'm a reporter. I know all the gossip, plus it's my job to know what's going on. Think about where we live, nobody can keep a secret around here."

Piper wonders what else Lindsey knows about Ethel and her death but isn't saying.

"You have a point there. Yes, I told the judge I would do it."

"What's the estate worth?"

"Gee, I don't know. I haven't seen it yet."

"Who did she leave everything to?"

"I know why you're a reporter now." Lindsey smiles at the compliment, but Piper's words aren't meant to be taken as complimentary. "She has a sister. Before you ask, no, I have not contacted her yet. The judge did give me the keys to Ethel's house, so I'm going to go over there after the shop closes and start taking inventory of everything in the house. What the sister doesn't want will eventually get auctioned off."

"You have to let me go with you."

"What? You want to come with me?"

"Yes, I want to know what's in the house."

Piper knows she could use the help but isn't sure if Lindsey is the right person for the job.

“I’ll agree to let you help me with the inventory. But you have to promise not to take any pictures and not write about anything we find until after the estate’s closed.”

“I promise,” Lindsey says with a smile.

“You can’t talk about anything we find in the house either.”

“Okay.”

“I mean it. I know how you like to talk.”

“Please, I’m not that bad.”

Piper doesn’t reply.

When a customer leaves and a table opens up, Piper goes outside and helps Mildred with her heavier than expected crocheting bag. When things die down, Piper gets an idea.

“Paul, can you manage this for me for a few minutes?”

“Sure.”

“I’ll be in the office if you need me.”

“No worries.”

Piper goes into the office and calls the sheriff.

After a few long minutes of being on hold, the sheriff answers, “Sheriff Abbott speaking.”

“Sheriff, it’s Piper.”

“What can I do for you, Piper?”

“I have someone here that could put good use to Ethel’s wheeled cart. If you don’t need it for evidence, would it be okay if I paid it forward and gave it to someone?”

“Oh, by all means.”

“Thank you.” Piper decided to ask another question. “Did you take anything out of the cart before bringing it into the coffeehouse that morning?” Piper knows that he did but she doesn’t know what. After all, she was appointed executor of Ethel’s estate and it’s her job to know where Ethel’s things are, even if it’s only a thermos. The sheriff confirms what Piper already suspected. The thermos was taken as possible evidence. “Do you know how Ethel died yet?” When he doesn’t answer she asks, “When are you going to announce it to the public?”

“Soon. As soon as it’s been confirmed.”

“I hope it’s soon. Someone’s been egging the coffeehouse ever since her death.”

“Why would they do that?”

“They think I’m responsible for her killing her.”

“Are you sure about that?” he asks.

“Pretty sure. The notes they left under the door said ‘MURDERER.’”

“Piper, why didn’t you tell me before now?”

“Because I thought as soon as you told the public she died of natural causes, all of this would end.”

“I see. Do you still have the notes?”

“Paul has both of them here at the coffeehouse.”

“I’ll send someone over to collect the evidence in a bit. Maybe we can get a handwriting analysis done on it.”

“If you’d hurry and announce how Ethel died, you may not need to analyze the note.”

Piper notices that the sheriff evaded the conversation about announcing that Ethel died of natural causes.

"I'll send a patrol car over in a bit."

"Fine."

"Bye, Piper."

"Bye, Sheriff."

Piper removes Ethel's things from the mobile cart and takes the cart out to the dining room. She parks it beside Mildred and sets her bag inside the cart before wheeling it a short distance.

Mildred watches her over her reading glasses.

"This works nicely," Piper says, parking the cart beside Mildred again.

"Mmm," Mildred mumbles before Piper leaves.

Piper thinks Mildred may be pleased with having a cart with wheels to carry her bag for her but with the scowl on her face, it's hard to tell. The scowl could be because the cart belonged to Ethel.

Piper walks back into the kitchen to the back door where she left Ethel's bag that was in her cart. Why would he take her thermos for evidence? She carries the bag to her office and removes everything piece by piece. In the bag she finds a shawl, a jigsaw puzzle, a couple romance books, and a 5x7 framed photo of a woman and a man. The photo is old and the couple in the photo is maybe in their thirties. They both look happy. Piper suspects it could be Ethel in her youth but it's hard to tell. She's never known Ethel to be married. Inside the cart is also a bottle of rose-scented perfume, and a broken empty locket.

Nearly an hour later, a police cruiser pulls up to the coffeehouse. Piper can hear the customers mumbling beneath their breaths. They probably think he's here to arrest Piper *and* Paul for the murder of Ethel Bowers. Before the officer can get out of his car, Piper runs the two notes outside to give to the deputy. She doesn't need the police to cause a scene or to give reason for gossip. Gossip is something Piper doesn't need.

Lindsey sticks around the shop until closing time. When Mildred leaves, Piper locks up and she, Lindsey, and Paul head to Piper's house to drop Paul off.

"Will you take Bailey out?" Piper asks as Paul is getting out of the car.

"Sure," he mumbles before closing the car door.

Piper and Lindsey head to Ethel's. They pull up out front of the house. It's a white side-by-side duplex with pale green shutters. Ethel lived on the right side and the left doesn't seem to have been recently occupied, at least according to what they can see from the curb. Lindsey's phone rings and she walks away so Piper can't hear the conversation. With Lindsey being a newspaper reporter, she's hears a lot of privileged information. Important information that someone like Piper isn't supposed to hear.

When she disconnects the call she says, "I sorry but I have to run, but can we do this tomorrow?"

"Sure. Tomorrow's fine."

Piper takes Lindsey to her car while she goes home and starts dinner.

CHAPTER 3

When they pull up at the coffeehouse, they see a police cruiser parked outside. Piper's first thought is something else has happened in Pineapple Grove and then she realizes that the shop wasn't vandalized last night.

"Look, Mom. They're watching the coffeehouse."

"I guess they are. I should have called Sheriff Abbott sooner."

Piper and Paul wave hello to the officer before walking into the coffeehouse.

It took a couple days for the sheriff to get the results back from the autopsy report and from the coffee that was found in Ethel's cart. The sheriff announces the cause of death at a press conference on TV at 10:00 a.m. The coffeehouse is packed with everyone but Lindsey as everyone listens intently to every detail the sheriff mentions on the TV news program.

The sheriff is sitting at a table along with the mayor and other law enforcement officers. "The cause of Ethel Bowers' death has been confirmed. It's with deep regret that we inform the public that there's a strong reason to believe she was murdered. The forensic team found traces of poison in Ethel's thermos. We're treating this as a murder, but we don't believe this is a serial killer type of murder. The public should not be in fear for their own lives as we strongly feel this is an isolated incidence. We'll update the public as more information becomes available. Anyone with any information is encouraged to come forward. That'll be all."

"Sheriff Abbott, do you have any suspects?" Lindsey asks, as she stands in the front row with her microphone in hand.

"I'm sorry. We're not taking any questions at this time." The television screen goes back to the previous show.

Piper knows the day Ethel died that Ethel didn't make it into her coffeehouse before Paul found her out back in the alley. But poison? Who would have poisoned an elderly woman? If a human ingests poison, do they die immediately? Or does it take days or weeks to kill a person? Can a single dose be enough? However, the town is talking and everyone has a finger to point.

As soon as the press conference is over, many of Piper's customers toss money on the counter and leave without saying a word. A few sit at the counter talking loudly and accusing Piper of poisoning the elderly woman.

"I had nothing to do with her death."

"Then why did she die in back of *your* shop?" a woman asks.

Before Piper and Paul can answer, everyone left sitting at the counter stands and leaves.

The nearly full coffeehouse is now almost empty. Mildred is the only customer remaining.

"Looks like we're closing early today."

Lindsey walks in and orders a hot tea. Piper imagines her coffee sales may plummet along with her doughnut sales.

"Piper, I know you didn't kill her," Mildred says.

"Thank you, Mildred."

"But, Lindsey, I can't say for sure you didn't kill her," Mildred adds.

Lindsey tosses her a look. “And why’s that?” What she really wanted to say could possibly have been held against her in the court of law someday.

“I saw you smiling the day they found Ethel dead in the alley.”

“I admit it. I was smiling at first, then I realized she was dead.”

“Always chasing that story, aren’t you, Lindsey?”

“Mildred, it’s what a good reporter does.”

“If you say so.” Mildred stands and pulls her dress out from her butt cheeks before she pushes Ethel’s cart toward the front door.

“Will you be in tomorrow?’ Paul asks.

“By the looks of it, I may be the only one brave enough to be here.”

Mildred leaves, and Piper knows that Mildred is right.

“Don’t listen to her. The townspeople don’t really think you poisoned Ethel.”

“Don’t they?”

“No, of course not.”

Piper looks at the wall clock. It’s just past 11:00 a.m. “When have you ever seen my business dead — I mean empty?”

Lindsey looks around at the bare room. “I can’t say I ever have.”

“It’s eleven o’clock and everyone’s gone. I have a feeling it’ll be like this until I clear my name.”

"Then I think we should work on that."

"What do you mean?"

Lindsey says, "Let's talk." Piper locks up, Paul walks home, and she and Lindsey sit down and talk. "If the police don't do something soon, your business and your reputation will be ruined."

"I know, but what can I do?"

"We need to solve this murder ourselves."

"I wouldn't know where to begin."

"First, we need to know the daily habits of Ethel Bowers."

"Okay, that sounds easy enough."

"What time did Ethel usually come into your shop?" Lindsey asks.

Piper thinks. "Usually, around nine, after the morning rush, and when she did come in that's when almost everyone in the shop took their cue and settled up their bill."

"I saw her at Sally's on Monday around ten when I was getting my hair done. I'd say it's safe to assume she went there directly after she left your coffeehouse on Monday."

"That sounds about right," Piper agrees. "As soon as I get home from work at two o'clock, I walk Bailey, shower, and make my way to the market. I usually see her in there refilling her thermos with Butcher Bob's free coffee."

Lindsey looks surprised. "You've seen her there after she accused Butcher Bob of trying to poison her?"

"Surprisingly, yes. I saw her there the same day the two were arguing here."

"About what time would you say that was?"

“I don’t know … four, maybe five. And if I remember correctly, Barb told me that they ran into her at the inn earlier that day.”

“Do you think that was before she made it to your shop or after?”

“If I had to guess I would say before. The inn’s close to Ethel’s house so I would think she may start her day there. Stephanie probably has coffee out pretty early for her guests.”

“Do you think Bob and Barb would stop by there that early?”

“I don’t know, but I think we should stop and talk to Stephanie. Barb said they were visiting her. If that’s the only place Ethel goes before she comes in my shop, that may be where the poisoned coffee came from.”

“Well, let’s start there.”

Piper and Lindsey make their way over to the inn to talk with the owner, Stephanie Guest.

“Good afternoon, Piper and Lindsey,” Stephanie greets them. “I didn’t figure you two would be hanging out together.”

“Let’s just say we have a common interest,” Piper says.

“Oh, yeah. What’s that?”

“Ethel Bowers.”

“Oh. I see. Very sad what happened to her. I watched the news conference this morning. Hard to believe someone would poison the poor soul.”

Lindsey remains quiet.

"Yes, it is," Piper says.

"Come on in so we can talk." Stephanie walks with them into the quiet bed and breakfast and they sit in one of the common living areas. "What's on your mind?"

"Lindsey has a story to write and I need to figure out how Ethel's coffee got poisoned. Since I have a coffeehouse, you can imagine what people are saying about me."

"I've already heard." Stephanie asks, "Would you like some coffee?"

They both immediately decline. "What have you heard?" Piper asks.

"It's not important. It's just gossip." Stephanie takes a sip of her coffee. "What can I do for you?"

"We're trying to learn more about Ethel's daily routine. We know that Ethel likes to take advantage of the free coffee wherever it's offered. Personally, I'm surprised she didn't die from a caffeine overdose. Would you be willing to tell us how often Ethel stops in here and fills her thermos with coffee?"

"You think I poisoned her?"

"No, not at all. We're just trying to find out Ethel's daily routine."

"Well, she stopped in here every day. Usually around the same time."

"What time was that?" Lindsey asks.

"Right around seven in the morning. I run breakfast from six to ten for my guests. She would come in for coffee and then leave."

"Since she was here during breakfast, would she also eat here?"

"She never sat down with the guests, but sometimes she would take a piece of fruit or a croissant with her when she left. I always offered for her to stay and eat but she never did."

"Do you know if this was her first stop of the day? Did she ever mention going anywhere else before she came here?"

"She never said, at least not recently. I know she used to say something about meeting someone on the beach some mornings. This was in the summer. She said they'd meet up for coffee and watch the sunrise together."

Lindsey asks, "Did she say if it was a man she was meeting?"

"No, she never said. I guess I never really cared enough to find out either. You know you could believe only half of what that woman said. All too often I'd believe the wrong half. I've heard her tell some tales, I tell ya."

"Haven't we all," says Piper. "Do you know of anyone who would want her dead?"

"Yeah, most of the town of Pineapple Grove."

Lindsey agrees. "Sadly, I think you're right."

"If you want to look someplace, you might want to start with Butcher Bob. That's where I would start if I cared enough to look into it."

"Maybe we'll do that. Thank you for your time."

Lindsey and Piper decide that is enough questioning for one day. They drive to Ethel's house so they can begin taking inventory and getting the place ready to sell.

When they pull up to Ethel's and get out of the car, they notice that the front door's ajar.

"Think the cops forgot to lock the place up?" Piper asks.

Lindsey shrugs her shoulder. "I hope it's the cops."

Piper pushes the door open and yells, "Hello." Nobody answers. "Is anyone in here?" she yells as she walks in. Still nobody answers.

They walk through the house together and see that it's empty of any intruder.

"The sheriff probably just forgot to close the door all the way. Nothing looks to be out of place."

Lindsey says, "Makes you wonder how good of a search the sheriff could have done, doesn't it?"

"It's not how it looks on television after cops conduct a search."

Lindsey laughs. "On *Law and Order,* they demolish a home looking for evidence."

"Obviously, not in Pineapple Grove."

They walk through the house and it's cleaner and cozier than the two expected. Ethel has plastic runners down on the carpet in what would be considered heavy-traffic areas. There probably wasn't much traffic as either Piper or Lindsey couldn't imagine anyone stopping by to visit Ethel. On the walls hang pictures of a much younger and happier-looking Ethel. To their surprise, a man is in most of the pictures with her.

"Who do you suppose that is?" Piper asks Lindsey.

"I've never known Ethel to be in a relationship."

"I think there may be something with this mystery man. Something's telling me that might be who she was watching the sunrise with," Piper says.

"I guess it could be, but if she was still seeing him wouldn't she have updated the pictures with more recent ones?"

"Maybe they split up and could meet only early in the morning. Maybe he's currently in another relationship with someone else. Or maybe it's with a new man and she didn't want it to be known."

"*Maybe* we're making something out of nothing," Lindsey suggests. They make their way into the kitchen. Lindsey looks over at Piper. "Have you been in the other half of the duplex yet?"

"Not yet. Let's walk through it and see if anything's over there."

"Sounds good."

Piper uses the same key they used for Ethel's house to open the door of the other side of the duplex. They walk through the other side of the duplex and see that it's minimally furnished with a couch, chair, a small dining table, a few dishes, towels, and washcloths, and a full-size bed and dresser. Someone could stay here in a pinch, but it isn't furnished enough for someone to call it home.

Ethel didn't keep any personal property of hers in this side of the house.

Piper and Lindsey go back to Ethel's house and decide to start in her bedroom.

Lindsey opens the closet door in the master bedroom and starts searching through the closet.

Piper gives Lindsey a notepad and a pen. “I’ll start looking through the drawers and tell you what’s in them. Then you write down what I tell you. Got it?”

Lindsey seems to be bored with this assignment already. “Got it.”

They go through the dresser drawers and then the nightstand. The jewelry box on the dresser looks to be the most valuable thing in the room. Piper’s surprised when she goes through it. It’s full of what appears to be real gold.

“Some of these pieces are quite nice,” Lindsey says, taking a ring out and placing it on her ring finger.

“They are. I bet these are real gold.”

“Do you think? I never saw Ethel wear jewelry.”

“I haven’t either, but this looks like real, not costume, jewelry to me.”

Piper places the jewelry box inside the closet for later. This may be something she’ll need to get appraised before the auction. She should also call Ethel’s sister to see what all she wants from inside the house first.

Next, they make their way back to the closet. Above the hanging clothes is a shelf with numerous shoeboxes, photo albums, and cardboard boxes. A few suitcases line the floor. While standing on her tiptoes, Piper reaches up and starts handing Lindsey several of the boxes. After she has everything cleared off the shelf, they both sit on the bed and begin the task of inventorying the contents of each box.

Most of the shoeboxes contain more photos of the life lived by a younger Ethel. In most of the pictures, Ethel looks to be around the age of thirty, maybe even forty. They don’t find any photos of her in her golden years. Whoever this man is, it appears that he played an important part in her life.

Some of the pictures are of them outside of a casino, at the river, having dinner together, and just relaxing at home.

Lindsey flips to a blank piece of paper and starts taking her own notes.

"Find out who mystery man is," she says out loud as she writes it down.

"Why does it matter who he is?''

"I just want to know."

"Always looking for a story." Piper looks away and sorts through another box of pictures.

"It's what separates a great writer from the good writers."

"If you say so."

Opening another box, Piper notices Ethel's tax forms from the previous several years. Piper pulls some out and starts reading it them.

"Looks like Ethel gambled from time to time," Piper says, handing Lindsey one of the most recent forms.

"It says she's won one-hundred-thousand dollars last year."

"That's quite a win, or series of smaller wins."

Looking around the room the two wonder what she did with her winnings. There's nothing new in the house and there's nothing worth one-hundred-thousand dollars, not even the jewelry.

They get to the last box and Lindsey opens it. It's an older shoebox, but it doesn't contain shoes or pictures.

“Um, Piper. You’re not going to believe this.”

“What is it?” Piper asks as she sits down the stack of pictures she was looking at.

Lindsey hands her the box. It’s filled to the top with one-hundred-dollar bills. “Money. A lot of money.”

Piper flips through the large stack of bills before picking up the stacks of money. “There has to be fifty-thousand dollars here. Why would Ethel have this much cash lying around the house?”

“Looks like we found her casino winnings.”

“I think we should call the sheriff?” Piper says, taking her cell phone from her purse.

“It’s not a crime to have money.”

“I know, but what if they killed Ethel for the money?” Piper asks Lindsey.

Lindsey turns on the bed so she’s facing Piper. “If they killed Ethel for the money, don’t you think they would have taken the money?”

“Maybe they couldn’t find the money.”

“If they had looked for it, they would have torn the house apart. It would look like a scene from *Law and Order*.”

“Good point. I’ll call Judge Greer and ask him what I should do with it.”

Piper calls the courthouse. After she has been placed on hold for several minutes, the judge picks up.

“Hello, Judge Greer speaking.”

“Liam, it’s Piper.”

“What can I do for you, Piper?”

“I’m here at Ethel’s. I brought a helper with me to help start taking inventory of the contents and we found a shoebox full of one-hundred-dollar bills. I’m not sure what I should do with it.”

Piper’s pretty sure he would want to know, especially since Pineapple Grove is a small community and he’s overseeing the estate.

“That’s a lot of money.”

“Her ten-ninety-nine tax form states she won it playing the lottery.”

“Count it and then take it to the bank. Open an account in the name of the estate. As you sell the property and the contents, just put it all in the account you set up for the estate. That way we can keep everything in one place.”

“Okay, sounds good.”

“Make sure to keep inventory of everything as you’ll get a percentage of the total profits in the end.”

“I will.”

Liam asks, “Have you contacted her sister yet?”

“No, not yet. I just got into Ethel’s house for the first time this evening. I plan on calling her this evening once I’ve gone through the house.”

“Sounds good.”

“I need to get off here so I can get to the bank before they close. I don’t want to have this much cash on me overnight.”

"If you're not comfortable transporting the money to the bank, I can have a deputy escort you."

Piper immediately thinks about her son being escorted by the police to the jail. Although it wouldn't be the same, she still doesn't ever want to have a police escort for anything.

"I have someone here with me so I think we'll be okay. I just wasn't sure what to do with the money."

"You did the right thing by calling. If you need anything else, I'll be here till about five."

"Okay. Thank you."

Piper hangs up.

"What did he say about the money?"

"Count it and take it to the bank."

"This should be fun. I've never counted this much money before."

They count the money not once but three times to make sure the amount is correct. After an hour of careful counting, they determined the amount to be exactly sixty-eight thousand dollars.

"I think this will be enough for one day. You need to add the sixty-eight thousand dollars cash on the inventory list we've started."

"Already did. I've never seen this much cash before in my entire life," Lindsey whispers.

"Me either."

Once outside the bank, Piper says, "I would ask you to keep this a secret, but when we open an account in the name of Ethel Bowers' estate and hand them sixty-eight thousand dollars cash, rumors are going to fly."

"Does that mean I can write about it?"

"No, you can't write about it. We had a deal, Lindsey. I'm worried if people find out for real that we found this much money, someone will burglarize the house."

"I know. Just thought I'd ask. You're going to bring me back with you tomorrow, right?"

"I'm sure you'll be hanging around the coffeehouse to make sure I do."

"That you can count on."

After they leave the bank, Piper takes Lindsey back to the shop where her car's parked before heading home. When she opens the door, Bailey's wagging her tail and looking up at her. Piper gets Bailey's leash and takes her out. After Bailey's walk, Piper showers before going out to the market to get something for dinner.

"Hi, Piper," Barb greets her from the other side of the counter. "Look, Bob, it's our second customer of the day," Barb says.

"Hello, Piper," Bob shouts from the back.

"Hey, Bob," Piper shouts so he can hear her. "You've had only two customers all day?"

"Sadly, it's true," Barb says. "Lindsey just left. Other than that, nothing. We think Ethel's murder has been bad for our business."

"You don't think it's because of Ethel's death, do you?"

"What else can it be? People think we poisoned her."

Bob comes out from the kitchen, wiping his hands off. “If business doesn’t pick up, we may be selling bad meat for real.” Piper shivers at the thought. “Bad joke. But we may be forced to close our doors.”

“My business is down, too.

“I heard.”

This didn’t surprise Piper. She knows people in Pineapple Grove love to talk.

She says, “As soon as they announced the cause of Ethel’s death this morning at the news conference, customers left the coffeehouse in a hurry. I guess I might be the prime suspect.”

“I might have to change my business to selling tea and crumpets if something doesn’t change.”

Bob gives Piper a sad smile.

She says, “As soon as they announced the cause of Ethel’s death this morning at the news conference, customers left the coffeehouse in a hurry. I guess I might be the prime suspect.”

Piper didn’t really believe that since she was never questioned about Ethel’s death. Well, not as a suspect anyway. They did talk to her and everyone else in the coffeehouse the morning Ethel died.

“Can they have two prime suspects?” Bob asks.

Piper didn’t know if he was serious, but she wasn’t about to ask. She couldn’t imagine Bob being a suspect either. She gets a pound of ground beef and heads home to make a meatloaf for dinner. Once everything’s mixed up and placed in the hot oven, Piper sits down to call Ethel’s sister, Abigail.

“Hello.”

“Hi, I’m looking for Abigail Bowers.”

“This is she. May I ask who’s calling?”

“My name’s Piper Armstrong. I’m calling in regards to your sister, Ethel Bowers.”

“Yes, the nice sheriff said someone would be contacting me.”

“First, I want to say I’m sorry for your loss.”

“Thank you. It’s very sad about my sister. I miss her already.”

“I’m sure you do. I’m appointed by the courts to be the executor of her estate. She wanted all her belongings to be sold off and the money given to you.”

“Do I need to do anything?”

“Not if you don’t want to. I’ve already been to her house. I don’t know if she has anything you may want to keep. I can hold off on selling anything if you want to take a look first.”

“I would like that, although there’s not much I need at my age.”

“When would you be able to come?”

“I just got out of the hospital. I can try to be there by the end of next week, if that’s not too late.”

“Next week’s fine. I’ll keep taking inventory, and when you come I’ll have a copy for you of everything in the house. You can keep whatever you want and then we’ll list everything else with an auctioneer.”

“That sounds great, thank you.”

"Oh, Abigail, there's one more thing."

"Yes, dear."

"I thought you'd want to know. We found a shoebox full of money."

Abigail sounds surprised. "Oh, really?"

"Yes. It was sixty-eight thousand dollars."

"Oh, my. That's a lot of money."

"Yes, it is. I took it to the bank and opened an account in the name of your sister's estate."

"That sounds like a good idea."

"I just wanted you to know. If I find anything else significant, I'll keep you posted."

"Thank you, Piper."

"Have you thought about funeral arrangements for Ethel?"

"Most of our friends and family have already passed. I'm having her cremated and will place her ashes on the mantel right beside Mom and Dad's."

This doesn't sit well with Piper, who has never not attended a memorial service for a deceased friend or relative. Even though Ethel wasn't her friend, Piper still thinks she deserves a memorial service.

"Would it be okay with you if I had a memorial service for her here at Pineapple Grove?"

Piper thought she could hear Abigail sniffle through the phone.

"My sister would've liked that."

"Would you want to attend? I could come and get you; maybe you could say a few words?"

"Thank you, dear. But I'm not well enough to make it this week. My doctor would never release me so soon after my surgery."

"Okay, I understand." Piper didn't know what else to say. "I'll be in touch."

"Thank you for doing this for my sister and me."

"It's my pleasure. Goodbye, Abigail."

Piper hangs up the phone and heads back in the kitchen to tend to her dinner.

~~~

The following morning Piper wakes up earlier than usual. Ideas for a memorial service for Ethel come to her mind. After she and Paul get dressed, they leave to prepare for the day at the coffeehouse. Piper isn't sure if they'll be busy or dead today.

After the doughnuts and coffee are made, Paul unlocks the door and turns the sign over from "closed" to "open." Like every other morning, Mildred's waiting outside.

Lindsey's the next person to walk through the door. Today, something seems different with her. She's more energetic than usual.

"Good morning, Lindsey," Piper says.

"You're not going to believe this," Lindsey begins. She reaches in her bag and pulls out the day's newspaper. After unfolding it she slides it across the counter to Piper. On the front-page it reads "Murder or Suicide in Pineapple Grove?" by Lindsey Miles. There was a picture of Ethel just under the headline.
~~~

“What’s this?” Piper asks. “You don’t think she consumed the poison willingly, do you?”

“I don’t think anything. It’s my job to present the facts to my readers and let them make their own assumptions.”

Piper reads the rest of the article. It ended with a comment from the sheriff saying as of now they’ll be investigating the death as a murder.

“Did you put the idea in his head that maybe Ethel consumed the poison of her own free will?”

“I did. It makes for a great story, doesn’t it?”

“It does. This might also help my business. Thank you.”

“It’s nothing. Just doing my job,” Lindsey winks.

“You don’t happen to have two of those newspapers, do you, Lindsey?” Mildred asks.

“I sure do. Here you go.” Lindsey stands and hands Mildred a newspaper.

“You’re a doll. Thank you.”

Lindsey sits back down at the counter.

“How did you persuade him into thinking maybe it was suicide?” Piper whispers.

“I’m not sure I did. But I did mention maybe she was depressed.”

Piper wonders if this was a possibility.

“You don’t think she consumed that willingly, do you?”

Piper can’t imagine anyone consuming poison willingly. There are easier and faster ways of committing suicide than ingesting poison.

Lindsey leans in and whispers so Mildred can't hear her. "All I know is I needed a story and this is my chance to prove myself as a writer. If the readers don't consider it a possibility, your business will be slow today. If they do consider it, and I hope they do, customers will be arriving shortly and the gossip will be ten-fold."

Just then the door opens and in walks some of Piper's regulars. They also happen to be some of the ones who rushed out of the coffeehouse after the news conference.

"Good job."

Lindsey crosses her long legs and smiles. "I know."

Paul leaves for his court hearing leaving his mother to manage the coffeehouse alone.

Business is steady and Piper stays busy. Just after ten o'clock, Piper gets a phone call from her daughter.

"What's up, Hannah?"

"Just wanted you to know that the sheriff just filed an affidavit for a search warrant."

Piper walks into the kitchen so no one can hear her conversation.

"A search warrant? To search what?"

"The home and business of Bob and Barb Stevens."

"Butcher Bob?"

"Yes."

"Oh, my. They can't be suspects, can they?"

"It's hard to believe either is capable of killing anyone. The judge just signed the warrant and the sheriff is on his way to their place now."

"What probable cause do they have to search the market and their residence?"

"That's something I don't know. People here aren't saying much."

"Okay, thanks for the heads-up."

"Mum's the word."

Paul returns from court and says he got sentenced to three days in jail.

Piper acts surprised although she already knew that Paul was going to get three days in jail.

Two hours after Hannah called, Sheriff Abbott was in the coffeehouse wanting to talk to Piper.

She walks with him into the kitchen.

"You went in Ethel's home yesterday. When you were there, did you find anything or see anything unusual?"

"Other than the shoebox full of money, no, nothing."

"You found a shoebox full of money?"

"Yeah. Ethel won some money at the casino last year. I called Judge Greer, he told me to put it in the bank under the Estate of Ethel Bowers."

"Did you find anything else?"

"Like what?"

"I'm sure you read the newspaper or heard from Ms. Miles this morning."

"She's in the dining room now. When she came in, she brought the newspaper with her."

"She's speculating that Ethel committed suicide."

"You don't think she did?"

"We're treating it as a murder."

Piper wants to ask about the search warrant, but she doesn't. "Do you have any suspects?"

"We do. When you were at Ethel's, did you notice anything unusual?"

"As a matter of fact, we did. The first time we went there the front door was opened. But I didn't notice anything out of place."

He gets a pen and small notepad from his pocket and writes something down. "When was this?"

"A few days ago."

"You said nothing looked disturbed?"

"That's right. The house was clean and everything looked to be in place. Of course, if something was missing, I wouldn't know."

"You didn't see anyone?"

"No. No one."

He jots down something else on the notepad. "Maybe they were looking for the money. It could be a motive." Piper isn't sure he's talking to her or to himself. "Do me a favor."

"Sure. Anything."

"Don't go back into the house today. I'm going to go over there myself when I leave here. You're not taking anything out of the house, are you?"

"The judge told me to take the money I found to the bank, but other than that, no. I'm just taking inventory. I spoke with Ethel's sister last night and she wants to take a look around before we start selling things off."

"That's a good idea. From now on, before you go into Ethel's house, I want you to call and have a police officer escort you into the house."

"Do you think that's necessary?"

"I do. At least until we know more about the case."

Piper didn't feel threatened, but maybe the sheriff knows more than she does.

"Okay. I will."

The sheriff leaves and Piper calls Lindsey into the kitchen and explains about needing a police escort to enter Ethel's house.

Paul asks, "Do you think it's safe for you to be there?"

"I do."

"Maybe I should start going over there with you?"

"No, Paul. We're fine. Thank you anyway."

Paul didn't like her answer. "Let me know if you change your mind."

Paul leaves the kitchen to wait on more customers in the dining room.

"Oh," Piper says, looking at Lindsey. "I forgot to tell you that I got ahold of Ethel's sister last night."

"And?"

"She wants to look around the house before we have the estate auction. While she's here, I plan on asking her about the man in all the photos."

“You think she’ll know who he is?”

“I think it’s our best chance of finding out.”

“We could also ask Mildred.”

“I never thought of that.” Before leaving the kitchen, Piper says, “You ask her. She seems to like you today.”

Lindsey walks over and sits down across from Mildred. Mildred stops crocheting and looks over her glasses at Lindsey.

“Mildred, have you ever known Ethel to be involved with a man?”

“No, why?”

“Well, when I was in her house I saw several pictures of her with a handsome young man. They both looked to be in their thirties so it was some time ago.”

“I never known Ethel to be involved with anyone. Ever.”

“They looked happy,” Lindsey adds.

“Ethel looked happy? I’d have to see it to believe it.”

~~~

Just before dinner, Piper decides to walk Bailey again. They walk longer and farther than normal. It’s a beautiful evening, and Piper feels bad about leaving Bailey cooped up in the house all day now that she has other duties to attend to.

She’d also like to get more involved in her photography but that’ll have to wait until after Ethel’s murderer is found.

The first stop on Bailey’s walk is Polly’s Print Shop to pick up the images Piper took of the girls the other day for their senior pictures. Polly’s been developing Piper’s photos ever
~~~

since she moved to Pineapple Grove. Polly also prints flyers, decals on t-shirts, and business cards. Just about anything you need, Polly will print it.

"Hey, I got your e-mail saying my prints are ready."

Polly searches for a large envelope with Piper's name on it.

"These turned out beautifully. The girls will love them."

"Thank you. I can't wait to see them."

Piper pays for her purchase.

Before Piper can leave, Polly has questions about Ethel's untimely death. Questions Piper can't answer but could easily speculate on. She tries hard to not partake in any conversation regarding Ethel's death.

"I heard that Butcher Bob poisoned Ethel. Do you know anything about that?" Polly says.

"What? Who said that?"

"I don't want to say, but I thought you might know something since she was poisoned in your coffeehouse."

"She *was not* poisoned in my coffeehouse."

"She was found out back in the alley. Same difference."

"That is not the same thing, and I hope you're not telling others that." Polly remains quiet. "If Bob poisoned her, why would he do it at my coffeehouse?"

"Because people won't suspect him, that's why."

Is Polly onto something? Are people suspecting Piper since Ethel died so close to her place of business? Why is no one suspecting she died of natural causes?

"What do you suspect, Polly?"

"Honestly?"

"Honesty would be nice."

"I think she was murdered and Butcher Bob did it."

Piper thinks this is ridiculous. "She was old. Don't you think she could have died from old age?"

"Nope. She was just saying she got a clean bill of health from Doc Simms."

Piper scans her memory and recalls Ethel saying those exact words.

"Why would Butcher Bob kill her? What does he have to gain from her death?"

"You're a business owner. Do you really need to ask that question?"

Call me stupid. "Yeah, I do."

"Ethel was telling everyone that Butcher Bob poisoned her. It had to be hurting his business as you need customers to thrive. With Ethel gone, the rumors will die right along with her and bam, his business is booming again."

Piper never considered this theory before. She likes Bob and his wife, Barb. Would they be capable of murder?

"Just because Ethel died in back of the coffeehouse doesn't mean the coffeehouse is responsible for her death. If Bob did poison her, a deadly dose would take time to get into her bloodstream, right?

"You have a point about that."

"People aren't accusing me of anything, are they?" Piper asks.

"I may have heard your name from time to time today."

Piper decides to leave it at that. Piper likes Polly, but she knows she's also a town gossip. Maybe moving to Pineapple Grove wasn't the best idea.

"Thank you for getting these done so quickly."

"You're welcome."

Polly gives Bailey a doggy snack before they leave.

Piper drops the pictures off at home before walking Bailey near the library when Bailey decides that is as good a spot as any to do her business. While Piper is waiting, she hears a female voice calling for her. She looks behind her and sees Harper Sinclair walking out of the library toward her. Harper is the town's librarian.

"It's funny how you can look everywhere for a person and then the next thing you know it's almost like they find you."

"You've been looking for me?" Piper asks.

"I have."

"I didn't think I was that hard to find as I'm at my coffeehouse every day from 5:00 a.m. to 2:00 p.m."

"And I'm here at the library from 10:00 a.m. to 6:00 p.m."

"Point taken." Piper asks, "What can I do for you?"

"I just heard you were placed in charge of Ethel's estate and you have access to her belongings."

"It's true. I was and I do."

"Ethel has a couple of my library books checked out and I was wondering if you would be a dear and return them to me."

"Sure, I don't see why that would be a problem."

“Thank you. It’s hard enough for me to get any money from the town to purchase new books so I have to keep the ones I have.”

“I understand. What books does she have?”

Harper reaches in her bag and pulls out a piece of paper. “I’ve already made a list for you.”

Piper unfolds the paper. “I think I recognize one of these books. Maybe it was in her cart the day she…” Piper doesn’t finish her sentence. “The property that was in the cart is at my shop so I’ll check tomorrow. The rest of the books I’ll keep an eye out for when I go back to her house.”

“Thank you, Piper.”

“You’re welcome.”

As Piper turns to leave, Harper says, “You know, Ethel wasn’t as bad of a person as everyone made her out to be.” When Piper doesn’t reply, Harper continues, “She was actually pleasant once she let her guard down. Getting her to let it down was a job, though. We both were in a book club together, you know.”

“A book club? No, I had no idea.”

“It’s true. We would meet a couple times a week on the beach. We’d drink coffee together and watch the sunrise. Most people watch the sunset, but it’s just as beautiful when it rises. Then we would talk about whatever book it was that we were reading at the time.”

“Wait. You’re the person Ethel met on the beach early in the morning?”

“Yes. You knew she was meeting someone?”

“Well, not until recently. I’m trying to figure out Ethel’s daily routine. Stephanie over at the inn told us that Ethel had mentioned to her that she would meet someone in the mornings, but she never mentioned who."

Harper says sadly, "I'm going to miss those mornings with her."

Piper gets an idea.

"Have you had dinner yet, Harper?"

"No, I haven't. I was just heading out to get something."

"I'd like to talk to you more about the book club and Ethel if you want to join me for dinner. I'll buy."

"Sure, that sounds nice."

"Why don't I drop Bailey off at home and I'll meet you over at the diner in ten minutes."

"Sounds good."

Piper speed walks Bailey back to the house. She opens the door and takes Bailey's leash off. Not wasting any time, she heads right back out the door to meet Harper.

When Piper arrives at the diner, Harper already has a booth and an order of loaded potato skins on the table.

"I hope you don't mind that I already started. I had to eat something. I was starving."

"No, I don't mind at all," Piper says as she grabs one of the skins and puts it on the saucer that's in front of her. "So, tell me more about Ethel."

"What else do you want to know?"

"Anything. I've always tried to like her, but she made it nearly impossible, even though she came in my shop every morning. She was never mean to *me*, but it just didn't seem like she could get along with anyone. The day before she died, she and Butcher Bob had it out in front of everyone because she thought he was trying to poison her. We all kind of blew it off, not believing someone would really poison her, but now she doesn't sound as crazy as we all might have thought she was."

"Well, you are right about that. Ethel was not crazy by any means. She was actually one of the most intelligent people I've ever met. She loved to read and she did mention to me that she thought someone was trying to poison her."

"Did she say who?"

Piper knows it is a stupid question the minute the words leave her mouth.

"If she had, I would make sure they'd be under arrest."

"Why did she think she was being poisoned?"

"She claimed she could taste the rat poison."

Piper knew that Ethel was poisoned, but she didn't know the type of poison was released to the public. More than ever, Piper wishes she had called Lindsey to be here with her. She is much better at questioning people than Piper is.

"Did you think she was being poisoned?"

"No. I thought something was off with her taste buds. If I had believed her, I would have taken her straight to the hospital, then I would have called the police."

"Rat poison? Are you sure she said 'rat poison'?"

"I believe so. Yes."

"How could she know what that would taste like?"

"I don't know."

They talk about Ethel through the meal and Piper gets a better understanding of who Ethel Bowers really was, but she doesn't learn anything useful that would help her in finding out who may have killed her. Harper doesn't know of Ethel ever being involved with a man. Harper has been a resident of Pineapple Grove for the last twenty-five years. Even though that seems like a long time, to an eighty-year-old it isn't all that long.

After they finish talking, Piper keeps her promise and pays for the meal and promises to keep an eye out for the books Ethel signed out of the library.

When Piper makes it back home, Paul tells her that Lindsey has been trying to get ahold of her. She even called the house phone so it must be pretty important. Piper feels for her cell phone and notices that she had left it at the house when she rushed out to meet Harper at the diner. She tries to return Lindsey's call, but doesn't get an answer.

Piper then makes several calls to see if someone can tell her what poison actually killed Ethel.

CHAPTER 4

The following day, Piper doesn't see or hear from Lindsey until she's walking Mildred out of the coffeehouse and preparing to lock up for the day.

"We have to talk," Lindsey says as she walks quickly behind Piper.

"Lindsey, I've been trying to reach you since last night."

"Well, looks like we ain't closing just yet," Mildred says, turning around to go back into the coffeehouse.

"Oh, but we are," says Piper. "You'll have to excuse us today."

"I may be old, but I know where and when I'm not wanted," Mildred says as she begins to walk off, pulling Ethel's wheeled cart behind her.

"It's not that we don't want you here, Mildred. We just have to tend to Ethel's estate. It's just boring stuff."

Mildred keeps walking and waves a hand over her head without looking back.

"Let's go into my office so we can't be seen." Once they get in the office, Piper says, "You're not going to believe this."

"I have news, too," says Lindsey. "You go first."

"So, while I was walking Bailey last night, we made our way over by the library and Harper was walking out. She wanted to know if we would look for some books that Ethel had checked out. She told me how Ethel loved to read. She seemed to genuinely like Ethel. They even had a book club."

"Boring." Lindsey pretends to yawn.

"Hold on, it gets better."

"It wasn't much of a club. It consisted of only the two, but guess where they met?"

"I don't know, where?"

"On the beach just before sunrise. They would drink coffee and watch the sunrise."

"So, she wasn't seeing a man?"

"Nope."

"Hmm. Interesting. You ready for my news?"

"No, I have more."

"Go on."

"Ethel suspected she was being poisoned."

"Harper told you this?"

"She said that Ethel said she could taste the rat poison."

"Rat poison? Did they release that information yet?"

"No, it was never mentioned."

Piper smiles and Lindsey sits up straighter in her chair. "You know something."

"I called a friend at the sheriff's office last night and they confirmed it was rat poisoning."

"You have someone on the inside?"

Piper says, proudly. "I prefer to call that someone an informant."

"Nice."

“Either Ethel really did suspect it was rat poisoning or Harper knows something very few people know.”

“This is interesting. Harper could be a person of interest.” Lindsey takes a pen and tablet out of her over-sized purse and jots down this new information. “Good job, Piper, but I already knew that Ethel was poisoned with rat poisoning.”

“How?” Piper asks.

“I also have an informant. The sheriff’s office just got the forensic report back last night. My informant said that the sheriff would be announcing it tonight on the news and it’ll be in the newspaper in the morning.”

“Wow. You’re good.”

Lindsey sets her pen down. “Are you ready for my news?”

“I thought that was your news.”

Lindsey laughs. “I have other news. Better new. Bigger news.”

“Sounds like it’s going to be interesting. What is it?”

“I found out who our mystery man is in the photos at Ethel’s house.”

“What!”

“It’s true.”

“How?”

“My photographer, Hunter.”

“Hunter? The guy who wears the bright shirts?”

“That’s him.”

“How would he know?”

“I overheard him talking to Stephanie at the diner about Ethel’s death. Stephanie mentioned to him about Ethel’s friend being poisoned many years ago. So, I’ve been looking through electronic newspaper articles at the newspaper trying to find a story that matched her story. After about an hour, I finally found the newspaper with the article in it and a picture of Carson Eubanks.”

“Who’s he?”

Lindsey pulls a photocopy of the newspaper article out of her purse and unfolds it before handing it to Piper “That’s Carson Eubanks.”

Piper reads the headline “Murder in Pineapple Grove,” and under it is a picture of the same man who is in the photos on Ethel’s wall. “I guess we found out who our mystery man is. Do you think the two murders are connected?”

“I didn’t at first. Then I read the article in its entirety.”

“Do I have to read it or are you going to tell me?”

“He was poisoned the night before he was supposed to marry Ethel Bowers.”

“What!”

“I swear. I couldn’t make this stuff up if I wanted to. And get this, they never found out who the killer was.”

“No!”

“Yes.”

“If we find who killed Ethel, I bet we’ll find who killed Carson Eubanks.”

“We need to get back over to Ethel’s.”

"About that. The sheriff wants us to call for a police escort before we enter Ethel's house. He told me to call him when we're ready to go in and he would have a sheriff's deputy go in with us."

"Better make that call."

Piper makes the call and the two leave the shop. When they pull up to Ethel's, a sheriff's car is waiting out front. Deputy Jace Keck gets out of the car and greets them. He checks both of their IDs before he walks in and makes sure the house is secure.

After several minutes he announces, "It's all clear," as he pokes his head out of the door.

Piper and Lindsey both walk in the house.

"How long have you been a cop?" Lindsey asks with a flirtatious smile.

"Go easy on the kid, Lindsey," Piper whispers.

"Oh, she's okay." Deputy Keck readjusts his duty belt and squares his shoulders. "Just about six months now. I'm still fairly new. I usually work in the jail, but they asked me to come over here to assist you gals."

"You going to keep us safe, Deputy Keck?" Lindsey asks.

"Yes, ma'am."

"To protect and to serve," Lindsey purrs.

"That's right. It's my sworn duty."

Piper starts to walk out of the room when she hears Lindsey ask, "Have you ever solved a murder, Deputy Keck?" Piper stops in her tracks because she knows where Lindsey's line of questioning will go next.

“No, not yet. Up until very recently, not much has happened in Pineapple Grove.”

“Do you want to?” Lindsey asks.

“I’m afraid I’m not on this murder case.”

“I’m not talking about this case.” Lindsey stands a little too close to the new deputy. It’s the first time Piper has actually seen Lindsey at work. She knows the rumors about Lindsey being slutty are just that, rumors, but watching Lindsey in action she can understand why someone would get the wrong idea about her. “I’m talking about a Cold. Hard. Case.” Piper knows she should walk away and not to be a witness to this, but her feet are frozen in place and she has a hard time looking away. Lindsey runs her hand down Deputy Keck’s uniform shirt, stopping just above his duty belt.

Deputy Keck swallows. Hard. “What case are you interested in?”

“Some thirty years ago a man named Carson Eubanks was killed in Pineapple Grove. Nobody was ever charged with his murder. We want to take a look at the investigation that occurred.”

“I don’t know. I could get into trouble taking things like that out of the department.”

“Who’s going to know? It’s a case that’s thirty years old. They haven’t looked at that case in so long they probably forgot all about it.”

“Sheriff Abbott wasn’t even a cop that long ago,” Piper says. “He probably doesn’t know the file exists.”

“Come on, Deputy Keck,” Lindsey pleads with batted lashes. Piper turns her head to keep from laughing.

"Please, just call me Jace."

"Okay, Jace. What will it take?"

Piper walks away. She doesn't want to be a witness to this part.

Deputy Keck thinks for a minute. "If you agree to have dinner with me, I'll see what I can do."

"Deal," Lindsey answers a little too quickly. "The file and a free meal. Sounds like a win/win to me."

Jace and Lindsey exchange business cards before he leaves.

Lindsey and Piper finish the inventory of Ethel's bedroom, the spare bedroom, and the upstairs bathroom before calling it a day.

"We're going to have a memorial service for Ethel."

"We who?" Lindsey asks.

"Me and you."

"That's news to me."

"I spoke to Ethel's sister and she's having her cremated."

"What's wrong with that? A lot of people cremate their loved ones."

"That's not what's bothering me. She's not having a memorial service for her."

"There's a good reason for that," Lindsey says. "Everyone in Pineapple Grove is considered a suspect. Who would come?"

Piper wonders if Lindsey isn't right about that.

"I don't know. But Ethel's dead and she needs a proper farewell."

"Even if we do have a memorial service for her, who would come?"

"I don't know." Piper considers this for a moment. "I'll plan something tonight and make the arrangements tomorrow, and we'll have it the day after."

"Once again, Piper," Lindsey says, standing. "Who'll come? Ethel didn't have many friends… if any."

Piper thinks for a moment.

"What if we have it at a place of business?"

"You mean like at the local market during business hours?" Lindsey laughs at the thought of Butcher Bob and Barb having Ethel's final farewell at their market. "I'm just kidding. But seriously, do you mean like at the coffeehouse?"

"No. That would never work. The coffeehouse is way too small. I was thinking about the library. Harper was friends with Ethel more than anyone. Maybe she'd like to host it?"

"So, your plan is to trick people to come?"

"I wouldn't call it that, exactly. But the library has the space and they seem to be busy."

Piper gets the jewelry box from Ethel's closet and walks to the front door. Lindsey follows.

"Just promise me you won't have it during the children's story hour." They walk outside and Piper locks up the house. "Make the arrangements and I'll be there."

"Good. I knew I could count on you."

"I'm off to the newspaper to write an article about the type of poison used in Ethel's death. If you need me for anything, call me."

"Thanks. I'll see you tomorrow."

On the drive home, Piper considers having the memorial service at the library but decides to have it at the church instead. She figures those who don't come will look suspicious and no one wants to be named the prime suspect even though there could be many.

She stops by the church to talk with the preacher before going home for the night. Thankfully, the preacher is more than willing and is very helpful with making the arrangements for Ethel's memorial service.

He is also helpful in making up flyers for Piper to pass around for shop owners to post in the place of business announcing the time and place for her memorial service.

Once Piper leaves the church, she calls Lindsey to see if she'll write a small announcement about Ethel's memorial service and place in the Pineapple Grove newspaper in the morning.

Next, she drives around town and passes out flyers to all the small businesses in the area.

~~~

The news conference and the newspaper article about Ethel being killed with rat poisoning stirs suspicion in the small town. Sheriff Abbott announced that the coffee in Ethel's thermos was laced with rat poison. Because of the type of poisoning used to kill Ethel, everyone's been asking Butcher Bob who the customers are who have been buying an excess amount of the product. The upside to this is the market's business is picking back up.

Mildred walks into the market and heads over to where the self-serve coffee stand used to be. It's now been replaced with a potato chip stand. Mildred asks Barb, "Where'd you
~~~

move the coffee?" Pulling Ethel's pull cart behind her, Mildred walks over to the counter where Barb is stocking the candy bars.

"We did away with it."

"Why?"

"Because of Ethel. Her coffee was laced with rat poisoning and we thought it would cut back on the suspicion of us looking guilty."

"It's a little late now, don't you think?"

Barb stutters. "I… I… I… guess so."

"Did you poison her?" Mildred asks.

Barb looks shocked. "Why, no. Of course not."

"Then you have nothing to worry about. It's just a matter of time before they find the killer."

"That may be true, but since her coffee was tainted, not many people have been rushing in here for the free coffee."

Mildred places her empty cup back into the cart. "I guess I need to get my coffee elsewhere."

"I'm sorry about the inconvenience, Mildred. Maybe once her killer's been caught, we'll offer free coffee again."

Mildred waves a hand over her head dismissing Barb. Before she leaves the market, she reads the notice about Ethel's memorial service on the bulletin board. She scoffs as she walks out of the store. Seeing that Mildred's dress is tucked in her underwear, Barb gives it a quick yank before anyone else notices.

~~~
~~~

Lindsey was up till the morning hours as she prepared the article about the rat poisoning and an article about Ethel's memorial service. When she finally gets up out of bed and gets her shower, there is a missed call and a message left for her on her answering machine.

"Hello, beautiful. Jace here." Lindsey's heart thudded at his smoothness. "I have what you're looking for. Meet me tomorrow night at The pub on the River for dinner *and* drinks."

Lindsey didn't need to hear the message again, but that didn't stop her from playing it over and over again. She thought it was very clever the way he didn't ask her out but more or less demanded it. She liked a take-charge kind of guy.

Bean There, Dunk That is busier than normal. Piper has heard from some of the early-morning customers that some of the small businesses stopped offering free coffee in their shops. She wonders if they have something to hide. She doesn't believe anyone in the small town is capable of murder, but she also knows someone is responsible for Ethel's death. Since she is fairly new to Pineapple Grove, Piper doesn't know anyone well enough to know who is capable of murder and who isn't.

Mildred sits in her seat crocheting as customers come and go throughout the day. Piper reminds everyone about Ethel's memorial service she is having for her at the church as she gives them their change after each purchase. When they show very little interest in attending, she announces, "We're having food after the service."

"So, you think the food will bring them to the service?" Mildred asks when the last customer leaves.

"I hope so."

Mildred places her yarn and crochet needle into her cart. She stands and yanks her floral dress free from her underwear.

“If you’re wanting people to come, I think offering food is a great idea.”

Piper’s eyes get big. This isn’t a compliment, but it’s close, and it may have been the nicest thing Mildred’s ever said to Piper.

“You do?”

“Sure,” Mildred says, refilling her cup with the last of the coffee in the carafe. “Who doesn’t love a free meal?”

“Does that mean you’re coming?”

“Sure. I’ll be there. I plan on wearing a rainbow of colors.”

Rainbow of colors? What does that mean? “You’re not wearing black?”

Mildred laughs. “No, black or dark colors are for mourning.”

“Mildred,” Piper says quietly, “you do know this isn’t a celebration, right?”

Mildred pulls her cart behind her toward the front door. “You call it what you want, and I’ll call it what I want.” And with that, she’s out the door.

Paul stands behind her as Piper could possibly be in shock.

“Don’t be surprised if she isn’t the only one dressed for a celebration.”

Piper gets a vision of a three-year-old girl’s birthday party. Bright-color balloons, pastel-color clothing, pretty decorated gifts and place settings. Piper can imagine that most people in town feel the same way as Mildred.

"Maybe this memorial service was a bad idea."

~~~

The next day, Piper, Paul, Hannah, and Lindsey decide it would be best to just make the food at the coffeehouse and transport it over to the church. Hannah, Paul, and Lindsey are not considered suspects, so this is the best option. Well, actually the sheriff didn't announce anyone as being a suspect, but that hasn't stopped the townspeople from speculating and forming their own opinions. Fortunately, they haven't lit torches, grabbed pitchforks, and executed those whom they think may be guilty. People still speculate that Piper is involved in Ethel's murder, but they also speculate that Harper, Sally, Stephanie, or Butcher Bob is also responsible.

Once everything is done, they load up Piper's car so she can take it to the church while everyone else goes home to change. Hannah offers to take Paul home for Piper.

Piper decides on a little black dress with black heels. She knows Hannah and Lindsey will also wear black and Paul will hopefully wear a dark suit. It is all common sense and Piper knows she doesn't need to tell her adult children or Lindsey what to wear.

Once the food is where it should be, Piper places a large framed picture of Ethel in the front of the room with a bouquet of fresh flowers. The picture is of a younger Ethel, but it still looks a lot like her. Piper is happy with her choice.

Just before 5 o'clock, Piper stands at the doorway of the church to welcome the guests. Well, she hopes there will be guests to welcome. The organ plays sad, soulful music.
~~~

Piper's shocked to see the first guest is Mildred. Mildred shows up wearing a bright yellow dress with a red hat and purple shoes. Piper tries hard not to stare. She greets Mildred warmly before handing her a pamphlet of the obituary with the Lord's Prayer written on the inside.

"Thank you for coming. You're the first to arrive so you can sit anywhere."

"You mean there'll be others?" Mildred asks snidely.

I hope so, Piper thinks to herself. "We're expecting a large crowd," Piper lies, stepping just outside of the church. She doesn't want to see what would happen if she tells a little white lie while standing inside the church. She'll need to ask for forgiveness later.

"That'll be the day," Mildred mumbles as she pulls her cart behind her. Piper notices that one of Mildred's stockings has fallen down her calf. She is grateful that her dress isn't tucked into her underwear as it has been on many occasions.

Piper's glad when Hannah, Lindsey, and Paul all show up at the same time. She is shocked to see what Lindsey's wearing. Paul and Hannah are dressed for the occasion.

"What are you doing?" she asks while giving Lindsey a stack of the memorial pamphlets to hand out to the guests.

"What?" Lindsey asks, adjusting the hem of her blue floral sundress.

"You look like you're dressed for a date, not a memorial service."

Lindsey smiles. "Great, because I have a date as soon as this is over with."

"What? With who?"

"Jace."

"Who's Jace?"

Lindsey smiles and hands a guest a pamphlet. "The deputy."

Piper suddenly remembers the deputy who was at Ethel's house. "You're seriously going out with him?"

"I am."

"I thought you were messing with him."

"Nope. I was dead serious."

"You're fast," Piper says, handing another guest a pamphlet. Lindsey clears her throat. "That's not what I meant," Piper corrects. "I meant the date was arranged quickly."

"I know, right. Jace called and told me where and when. Who am I to argue?"

"Can you meet me back at Ethel's after your dinner date?"

"I sure will."

She focuses her attention on the guests and the array of colorful clothing they chose to wear for Ethel's memorial. Was Mildred right? Did these people just come for the food? Is anyone sad about Ethel's passing?

The librarian shows up in a black dress, a black hat, and black heels. Harper's nose is red from crying. She hugs Piper at the door. "Thank you for doing this for Ethel."

"It's our pleasure. We're glad to be able to do this for her."

"I hear the rumors going around, and I know there's no way you could have poisoned Ethel."

Piper feels like this is a slap in her face, Piper knows exactly how to reply.

"Just as I know you couldn't have killed her either."

Harper nods. She knows she deserves that.

"I was going to have a prayer or something at the library as I didn't think this many people would have attended." She looks around the nearly full church. "How did you get so many people to attend? Even the sheriff and the judge are here," Harper says with a surprised tone in her voice.

"I guess more people liked her than even we knew."

Paul says, "We're having food afterwards."

"I understand now." Harper looks around the room at all of the bright colors. "Looks like a celebration of sorts."

"It's a celebration of Ethel's life," Hannah lies.

Piper is happy that Hannah came up with such a convincing lie so quickly, but she wonders how she could do that at such short notice.

"I suppose."

Harper takes a seat and Piper, Lindsey, Hannah, and Paul follow. The preacher gives a heartfelt service. He's known Ethel for many years so he is able to say some personal things about her. The only person in the room crying is Harper.

The preacher thankfully doesn't ask if anyone wants to stand and say a few words about Ethel. Even he knows how the townspeople feel about her. Piper can imagine what the people would have to say about Ethel. Well, maybe since the sheriff is there they'd be on their best behavior, but that is a chance no one is willing to take.

Lindsey leaves right after the service. Piper wants to tell her to get some good information from the cold case of Carson Eubanks, but Lindsey leaves before anything could be said. Butcher Bob and Barb also leave immediately after the service. Piper isn't surprised. Maybe he still has some cleaning to do to ensure the rat poison is gone from his home *and* his business.

Piper didn't really believe that, did she? However, she still doesn't know what the probable cause was the sheriff had to issue a bench warrant on Butcher Bob's place of business and residence. She may never know as the sheriff, Butcher Bob and Barb may be the only ones who know the answer to that question. She also doesn't know what they recovered, if anything. She does know neither Bob nor Barb was arrested. Could it be the police are still testing whatever they found? Is that why Butcher Bob and Barb stopped offering free coffee? Did the sheriff confiscate the self-serve coffee station? Piper thinks she needs to call her informant to get the info.

The food is served buffet style. Piper, Paul, and Hannah sit beside Mildred. Paul offers to get Mildred's plate for her while he gets his own.

"Paul," Mildred whispers, leaning forward as if she's going to tell him a huge secret.

Paul also leans in. "What is it?"

"You don't have a little something extra I can add to my coffee, do you?" Paul thinks she's making a bad joke about rat poison when he realizes she's talking about alcohol. "I need a little something to get me through dinner." As much as Paul wishes he had something to take the edge off, sadly, he doesn't. "Never mind. I have a feeling the preacher may frown on us drinking in the house of worship."

"I think you may be right." Paul stands to leave.

"Mildred, behave," Piper demands.

"Don't act so surprised. He probably tipped the bottle before walking in here today."

It's rarely that Piper's left speechless but this is one of those times. She wonders why she sat down with Mildred. She also wonders why Mildred is being so mean. Piper watches as Mildred crochets her blanket and acts as though she didn't just insult Piper's only son.

Paul brings back two plates of food and sets one down in front of Mildred. "Can I get you some more coffee, Mildred?"

Piper is happy to see that her son holds no ill feelings toward Mildred for her most recent jab at him about his drinking.

"That would be nice, dear."

Piper's shocked at the way Mildred's speaking to Paul. It's as if Mildred can't remember insulting him just a few moments earlier. Maybe she suffers from memory loss that no one knows about. Piper knows for sure Mildred suffers from mood swings.

~~~

Lindsey makes sure she shows up for her date a little late. She wants to see Jace squirm at her tardiness. Surprisingly, he looks relaxed while sitting at a two-top table in the center of the restaurant. He stares in appreciation as she walks across the room. She's surprised to see he's wearing a suit and tie. She's always loved a man in uniform, any uniform. But a man wearing a suit holds a special place in her heart. He stands as she nears the table.

"You look stunning," he says, pulling her chair out for her.
~~~

The first thing Lindsey wants to do is ask him if he brought the cold case file, but she finds his comment flattering and wants to bask in his affection, first.

“Thank you. You look pretty handsome yourself.”

He smiles as he takes a seat across the table from her.

“Thank you. There’s a pretty woman I’m trying to impress.”

Lindsey thinks it is funny how he’s talking about her in third person. She decides to play along.

“I don’t know who the woman is, but I’d say you succeeded.”

The server comes up and takes Lindsey’s drink order. Jace already has a martini sitting in front of him.

“So, did you bring the file?” Lindsey asks when the server leaves.

“Can we enjoy dinner before we get down to business?”

“We can, but I don’t see the file.”

“It’s because I don’t have it.”

CHAPTER 5

Lindsey isn't sure what to think of Jace's comment. She agreed to have dinner with him, and he agreed to get the cold case file for her to review. She's wants to remind him they had a deal — dinner for the file — but she doesn't like the way that sounds in her head.

"Why? Where's the file?" she asks. "Is the file locked away in the archives?"

"Actually, it was pretty easy to find. Nonetheless, I wasn't able to bring the file outside of the department, but I did have a chance to review it and you'll be surprised at what I found."

"Do tell," says Lindsey as she leans closer to the table.

Jace mimics her movement. "It's believed that Mr. Eubanks was poisoned at the local pub. A Maverick Smoker owned the pub back then. However, it's no longer a pub; it's now our local inn owned by Stephanie Guest."

"Is this Smoker guy still around?"

"He moved away after he sold the pub. And he sold the pub shortly after the Eubanks' killing."

"Could it be possible that he poisoned Carson and moved away once he was cleared?"

"That's the thing I don't understand," Jace says. "He was never listed as a person of interest. So, I'm not sure why he would have just up and sold the place and left town."

"Maybe his business took a nose dive after the killing?"

"That's very possible."

"Did they ever have a person of interest?"

The waitress brings Lindsey's drink and their salads before leaving.

"They did. The current owner of the inn was a person of interest."

"Stephanie Guest?"

"That's right. According to the file, she was questioned several times about the murder, but was never charged. I'm still looking for copies of the tapes from the interviews, but I haven't had any luck thus far."

"Now that I think about it, Stephanie didn't seem too sympathetic about Ethel's death either. Not saying she was wrong about everyone not liking Ethel, but who admits to wanting someone dead. That kind of hatred comes deep within the soul."

"From what I've witnessed, not many people were concerned about Ethel's passing."

Lindsey doesn't know Stephanie very well and she wonders if Stephanie could have killed Carson Eubanks or Ethel Bowers. What motive could she have?

"I think I want to go stay at the inn," Lindsey says.

"What's wrong with your place?" Jace asks.

Lindsey's eyes get big when she realizes how this must sound to Jace and that's not what she meant. She's afraid Jace might think it's a proposition and it isn't.

"I think Stephanie Guest may know something. I just want to look around the place. See if I can find anything that looks suspicious."

"You'll have to keep me posted."

"I will."

"If we're done with business, I'd like to enjoy my meal with my beautiful date."

Lindsey blushes. "You're just full of compliments this evening."

Jace smiles. "I'm just warming up."

The rest of the dinner feels like more of a date than a business meeting. There's no more talk of cold cases or unsolved murders.

After dinner, Lindsey and Jace meet Piper back at Ethel's. After Jace checks the inside of the house, the three make their way to the dining room table. Lindsey and Jace bring Piper up to date with what he found in the Eubanks' file.

When Piper is caught up on Carson's murder, Jace leaves and Lindsey and Piper go into the kitchen to continue their inventory there.

Piper bends down to pick up a button off the floor. "Does this look like it belongs to something you would wear?" Piper asks.

"That's an odd orange color for a button. I already know that it's not mine."

Piper inspects the button. "It's not mine either."

"There's a whole jar of buttons in the second drawer," Lindsey says, pointing to the cabinet drawer by the kitchen sink.

Piper opens the drawer and carelessly drops the button inside before closing the drawer.

Jace leaves and Piper clears out the refrigerator while Lindsey boxes up the canned foods in the pantry before calling it a night.

That night, Piper takes the canned food and donates it to a shelter, while Lindsey rushes over to the inn to check into a room for the night. She suspects Stephanie's involved with Ethel's murder and she plans to prove it. But first, she'll need some hard, solid evidence.

Stephanie suspects Lindsey is up to something but she doesn't know what. She figures it has to do with Ethel's murder. She thinks that Butcher Bob should be getting more attention than she is, seeing how Ethel actually accused him of trying to poison her right before her death.

In the morning, Lindsey comes down for breakfast before checking out of her room.

"Did you sleep well, Lindsey?"

"I did. Thank you."

A guest comes down the stairs, walks past the breakfast room, and goes straight to the registration desk.

"Please excuse me while I check out a guest."

Lindsey sits at the table and wonders where someone would store rat poison in their home or in their business. The basement and garage come to mind. What excuse would Lindsey have to search Stephanie's basement or garage? Nothing that she can think of right now. She'll need a better plan. Just before Lindsey checks out of the inn, she uses the restroom on the main floor. She searches under the sink, the medicine cabinet, and then the linen closet before she finds what she's looking for. Bingo. There it is in plain sight. Lindsey gets excited when she realizes that she possibly just solved a murder case on her own. She stuffs the rat poison into her oversized handbag, says a quick goodbye to Stephanie, and then she quickly checks out of the inn.

As soon as she's in the car, she calls Deputy Jace and he agrees to meet her at a local diner. Lindsey's convinced that Stephanie has to be Ethel's killer and quite possibly Carson Eubanks' killer, too. It's too big of a coincidence for her to have bought the pub where Ethel's fiancé died and then later to have turned it into an inn. Then she just happens to have the same type of poison that Ethel died from several days earlier in her bathroom closet.

Lindsey arrives at the diner before Jace does so she sits at the booth drinking coffee anticipating his arrival.

Jace walks through the door several minutes later and takes his seat across from Lindsey.

"What's on your mind, beautiful?"

"You know how I told you that I wanted to stay at the inn and look around?"

"I do."

"Well, I got a room and stayed there last night. I used the restroom on the ground floor this morning and I found a box of rat poison in the linen closet. She wasn't even trying to hide it."

"I see. What did you do?"

"What do you think I did? I took it," she says as she grabs the box of poison from her handbag and places it on the table.

Jace grabs the box of poison off the table and quickly places it next to him out of view of others.

"You can't just advertise this stuff. Do you think anyone saw you snooping around at the inn?"

"No, the inn was empty when I went into the bathroom."

"You have to be careful, Lindsey. We're dealing with a murderer here. These people are dangerous and I don't want anything to happen to you."

"I can take care of myself."

"I'm not saying you can't, but you should leave this to law enforcement."

"We should talk to the sheriff and tell him what I found."

"Lindsey, I need to tell you something first."

"Okay, what is it?"

"If you would have conducted a little more research, you would have found that the town of Pineapple Grove has had a problem with mice *and* rats for many years. Every business around here that sells or offers food is going to have rat poison somewhere on their property."

"No way."

"I'm sorry. It's true. If you don't believe me, you should ask your friend Piper. I'm sure she has a box of rat poison in her home and her business as well."

"Oh," says Lindsey. "I'm sorry. This is embarrassing. I was so sure that Stephanie had something to do with the murder that I wasn't thinking well enough."

Lindsey has never had a reason to purchase rat poison, and she's never noticed a problem with rats or mice.

"It's okay. I think it's cute how you want to solve this murder to help your friend's reputation."

"You do?"

"Very much so."

~~~
~~~

Piper's surprised and somewhat glad when Lindsey doesn't show up at the coffeehouse today. She figures Lindsey's going through more newspaper articles or something else related to Ethel's death is consuming her time. Could it be possible she's spending more time with the deputy?

Today, Piper wants to pay a visit to Hunter Gallagher's mom. She knows Stephanie won't tell her anything, but maybe Hunter's mom will since she was alive at the time of Carson Eubanks' murder.

After the coffeehouse closes, Piper heads home first to take Bailey out. She showers and changes before heading to the Forever Young nursing home. Paul left to serve his three-day jail sentence earlier today.

When she walks in, she heads straight to the nurse's station and the nurse directs her to Mrs. Gallagher's room. It isn't until Piper's walking into the room that she learns that Mrs. Gallagher's first name is Ruby. A laminated paper is framed outside of her room with the details of Ruby's life listed in two short paragraphs. Piper thinks it's sad that a sixty-five-year-old woman's life can be summed up in two short paragraphs.

Piper stops and takes the time to read about Ruby's life before entering her room. She learns Ruby was born and raised in Pineapple Grove and is the mother of six children. All but one of her children have moved away. She's worked as a waitress, a teacher, and lastly a caregiver.

After Piper finishes reading about Mrs. Gallagher, she walks into Ruby's room. Ruby sleeping peacefully in her bed. She looks younger than Piper had expected. The note on the door said she is sixty-five years old. Piper wonders what could have happened to Ruby for her to be required to stay in a nursing home at such an early age. Maybe she's suffered a stroke or heart attack. Or maybe she suffered injuries from the car accident that claimed her husband's life.

Piper quietly looks around the room and notices several family pictures hanging up. There's also several books and a pair of eyeglasses on the nightstand. A calendar's hanging up and it appears that her guests sign it on the day that they visit. Piper looks over the calendar and is pleased to see Hunter visits his ailing mother often. So do people named Milly, Sandy, Mike, Beth, and Bob. Maybe they're friends of Ruby.

She doesn't plan on waking the sleeping woman, thinking she'll return later this evening to speak with her. But when she turns around to leave, she bumps into the bedside table, jarring her awake.

Ruby opens her eyes and says, "Can I help you?"

"I'm sorry to wake you, Mrs. Gallagher. I just stopped in to see you."

"It's okay, but do I know you?"

"No, you don't. My name's Piper Armstrong, and I own a coffeehouse here in town. Your son works with my friend."

"What does that have to do with me?"

"I was wondering if you can remember anything about Carson Eubanks?"

"Why?" She reaches over and puts on her eyeglasses. "That's much better. Are you a reporter?"

Piper just told her she owned the coffeehouse. "No. I own the coffeehouse here in town."

"That's right. I remember you telling me that." Piper just smiles. "What is it you want to know?"

“Whatever you can remember about the night he died.”

“I do remember the whole town was in shock. Things like that just don’t happen around here.”

“Do you remember if they had any suspects?”

“Yes. Yes. They had a suspect.”

Piper waits for Ruby to tell her who the suspect was but Ruby remains quiet. “Do you remember who it was?”

“Who what was?”

Piper thinks this could be a waste of time since Ruby’s memory’s fading. “The suspect?”

“I know they questioned a girl named Stephanie, but she was never charged.”

“Did anyone in town suspect anyone?”

“Everyone in town suspected someone. But I always thought it was Ethel.”

Piper thinks to herself, *Finally, we’re getting somewhere. As long as Ruby can stay focused.*

“Why would Ethel want to kill the man she was set to marry?”

“If I knew the answer to that, I might be a suspect.” Piper just smiles.

“Were you there that night Carson was killed?”

“Are you a police officer?”

Piper has already told Ruby she owned a coffeehouse twice and she doesn’t want to mislead Ruby into thinking she is a sheriff’s deputy investigating a murder. Piper knows for sure that people get arrested for impersonating a law enforcement officer. “No. I own a coffee and doughnut shop here in Pineapple Grove,” Piper reminds her.

“That’s right, you already told me that.” Ruby adjusts herself in her bed. “I was there that night for a little while.”

“And they never made an arrest in his murder?”

“That’s right. When they couldn’t find out who did it, the sheriff made it seem like Carson poisoned himself.”

“Was he suicidal?”

“Who?” Ruby asks.

Piper inhales deeply. She hopes Ruby’s memory’s intact. “You just said that the sheriff thought Carson Eubanks poisoned himself. Do you remember if Carson was suicidal?”

“I didn’t know him very well.”

Piper decides this is enough for one day.

“Thank you for your time. Can I get you anything before I leave?”

“No, dear. I’m fine.”

Piper leaves more confused than ever. She heads over to the police station. She’ll use visiting her daughter, Hannah, as an excuse to hopefully run into the sheriff. She hasn’t heard anything about the search warrant they executed on Butcher Bob and Barb’s house and the market. Piper’s anxious to see if they found evidence indicating that they murdered Ethel. Of course, if there was conclusive evidence, they would have already made an arrest and it would have been all over the news. The whole town of Pineapple Grove would be talking about the arrest or arrests.

Pineapple Grove is a small, tight community. Neighbors murdering neighbors doesn't happen here, does it? Who hated Ethel enough to want to kill her? She doesn't know, but she's determined to find out.

She gets out of the car, squares her shoulders, and walks into the sheriff's department. She greets everyone she knows as she makes her way to the records room where Hannah works. Hannah's sitting at her desk with headphones on, dictating reports of a car accident that happened a few days prior.

Piper waits patiently for her daughter to finish or to notice she's standing at the open service window. It doesn't take long for Hannah to see her mother watching her. With a huge grin, she removes her headphones and says, "Hey, what brings you down here?"

"I thought I could take my daughter to dinner."

"What time is it?" Without waiting for her mother to tell her, Hannah looks at her watch and then she looks around the empty room. Everyone else has already gone for the day. "It's late."

Piper laughs while scanning the hallway for the sheriff. Maybe he's gone for the day, too. Her daughter diligently worked right through quitting time. It's no wonder that Hannah is such an asset to this place. It's good to know that her hard work and dedication haven't gone unnoticed. She's not only been recognized as employee of the month, but also employee of the year. Hannah wraps the cord around her headphone, shuts down her computer, then turns off the lights and locks the doors. "Dinner sounds great. What do you have in mind?"

"I need a drink. I thought we could get something at the new pub that recently opened down by the river."

"Sounds great."

Piper smiles at her beautiful daughter. "Good. I'll drive."

Once they're both buckled up in the car, Piper pulls out of the parking lot. "You said you needed a drink. Is everything okay?"

"It's fine. Just lots of gossip going around about Ethel's murder. I'll be glad when they find the person or persons responsible."

"It gives me goosebumps thinking about someone poisoning that little ole lady."

For the first time Piper considers the effect this murder has had on her daughter. "Are you scared they could strike again?"

"Unless they're caught, what's to stop them from adding rat poison to any of the free coffee canisters setting out in the local businesses?"

Hannah has a point. That's why many of the local shops stopped offering free coffee to their patrons.

"Would you feel safer if you moved back into the house with me and Paul?"

Hannah laughs. "No. I might consider that if Paul weren't still living at home."

Piper knows how much Hannah and Paul fight. She also knows they love each other, but that doesn't stop the fighting between the two.

"He's rarely there."

"Thanks, but no thanks. Besides, I'm too old to be living with my mom."

"I didn't realize there was an age limit." Piper smiles. "There's an extra bedroom if you ever change your mind."

Hannah looks lovingly at her mother. "You're not scared, are you, Mom?"

"I wouldn't say I'm scared. But I'll be glad when they find the person or persons responsible." This is a good time for Piper to ask about Butcher Bob. "You didn't hear if they found anything at Bob and Barb's, did you?"

Hannah knows that most things she hears inside the sheriff's department are privileged information. But she also knows that this information will be announced to the public soon.

"Other than rat poison, there wasn't anything linking the two with her killing."

Rat poison is common for any business owners to have in their garages or cleaning closets. Because Pineapple Grove is near the water, rodents are a common nuisance. Rat poison is about as common as someone having mothballs in their closets.

"For the sheriff to get a search warrant, he had to have probable cause. You wouldn't know what that was by any chance, would you?"

"That I don't know. But what I do know is Barb and Bob are cleared — so far — of any wrongdoing in the murder of Ethel Bowers."

"Do they have any other suspects?"

"I don't know that either. If the sheriff suspects someone, he's pretty quiet about it."

Piper doesn't want another cold case murder in Pineapple Grove. She and Lindsey will have to step up their game to find the killer at large.

The pub is quaint and has an island feel about it. With the wind blowing Hannah's hair in the breeze, she inhales the fresh air.

Piper says, "I feel like I'm on some tropical oasis."

"Me, too. Tell me again why we've never been here before?"

Picking up a plastic menu, Piper hands one to her daughter. "Because I think they just opened, didn't they?"

"That's right. I think it's been only a few weeks."

A good-looking man comes up and takes their drink order. He's probably about Piper's age. "I'm a little short staffed this week so please forgive me for the wait."

Piper smiles. "We just got here."

He looks around the busy establishment and smiles. "Good. I must be caught up." Piper isn't sure if he's kidding or not, but the comment makes her smile. "What can I get you to drink?"

Piper had wanted a draft beer, but after browsing the drink menu she decides on a Bahama Mama cocktail instead.

"Excellent choice and what about you?" he asks, looking at Hannah,

"The same for me as well."

Someone calls for "Banks" and the man answers with a wave. "If I don't find another server in a few days, I'm going to change my name. Look over the dinner menu and I'll be right back with your drinks." He looks around the busy room. “Maybe not right back, but I promise I’ll return with your drinks sometime this evening.”

Piper laughs and he turns to leave the table.

“I think you might like him,” Hannah says, picking up the dinner menu.

“He’s funny.”

“And good looking.”

“I noticed that, too.”

They each browse the menu as they want to have their dinner order ready when the server returns. Thankfully, they don’t have to wait that long for the cold beverage.

“Two Bahama Mamas for the ladies. Have you decided on your dinner yet or do you need more time? I’m in no hurry as it looks like I may be here well into the early morning.” Piper laughs again, and he offers her a friendly smile. “Finally, someone who gets my sense of humor.”

“I think you’re hilarious.”

The man bows. “Thank you. I’ve been working on this routine for some time.”

“It’s a routine, is it? Here I thought it was spur-of-the-moment talent.”

“Another compliment from the lovely lady?” Piper blushes. “I think I might like this serving gig after all.”

“You should. You’re quite good at it.”

“Don’t give me too much credit, there’s still room for error.” Piper laughs again. “Are you both ready to order or do you want to enjoy your drink first?”

“We’re ready,” Hannah says.

“Great. So am I.” Piper and Hannah wait for him to get his pen and pad ready to write down their orders, but it looks like he may do it from memory. “What have you decided on?”

“You don’t want to write it down?”

“Nah, I prefer not to. I like to be just as surprised as the customers are when I bring out their food. Sometimes they get what they order, sometimes they don’t. Tonight, it’s been hit and miss.”

Piper and Hannah both laugh.

“I’m going to have the fish and chips.”

Piper says, “I’ll have the same.”

The man takes the plastic menus. “Are you ordering the same thing to make it easy on me?”

“Yes,” they reply in unison.

Now he laughs. “Thank you. I can appreciate that. I shall return, I hope.”

When he leaves, Piper says, “He’s hilarious.”

“He is pretty funny. I guess you need to be when you’re working in this environment.”

“I guess.” Piper sips her drink. “Banks. That’s a strange first name for someone.”

Hannah looks at her mother. “Piper’s a strange first name, too.”

“Point taken.”

“It’s probably short for something or maybe it’s a nickname.”

“Maybe he’s wealthy and this is a name his friends gave him,” Piper teases.

“Or he got this name after buying the pub on the river.”

“You mean like river banks?”

Hannah laughs. “Exactly.”

“I think you’re funny, too.”

“And I think you had too much to drink.”

Not yet, Piper thinks to herself.

Piper and Hannah enjoy the calypso music as they people-watch. Piper can’t recall the last time a server was this entertaining. Most servers are much younger than their server is. She wonders whether he’s the host or perhaps the owner since he said he’s short staffed. The pub is much more relaxed than other places in Pineapple Grove and it’s a great change from the stuffy restaurants they usually frequent.

“Since they’re looking for help, maybe Paul should apply here for a serving position. They look busy enough, and he might just make enough to move out of your house and into something of his own.”

Piper knows she’s right about Paul getting a job and moving out, but she isn’t sure that working in this kind of an establishment is the right place for him.

“I’m not sure this would be a good idea.”

Hannah looks around at the overly large cabana-style bar. “Yeah, you’re probably right. I can see him staying plastered if he worked this closely to alcohol.”

Piper can’t argue with her, so she remains quiet about Paul working in a pub environment. She doesn’t think Paul’s an alcoholic, but she can't deny he drinks too much on occasion.

"Paul went in this afternoon to do his mandatory three days in jail."

"I know. I saw his name on the jail roster this afternoon."

Before the conversation gets too deep, Banks returns with some tortilla chips and salsa and sets it in the middle of the table. "For you."

Hannah looks at her mom as if to say, "We didn't order this."

Piper must have read her mind, but she didn't correct the waiter. "Thank you."

Banks smiles. "No, I didn't mess up your order just yet. These are on the house. Every table gets some."

"Oh," Hannah says, sitting up to dip the tortilla into the mild salsa. "In that case, thank you, again."

"Don't thank me. It's a smart way for the owner to increase his bar sales. The more of the salty chips you eat, the thirstier you become. Just wait. This won't be your only drink."

Piper and Hannah both laugh. "That's a great idea. Maybe the owner can give my mom some tips to increase her sales."

Banks looks over at Piper. "Are you Mom?"

"I am. Hi, I'm Piper Armstrong and this is my daughter, Hannah."

"It's nice to meet both of you."

"It's nice to meet you, too."

“What business do you own?”

Someone calls for Banks, but he ignores it this time.

“I own Bean There, Dunk That. It’s a coffee and doughnut shop over on Coconut Creek.”

“I know it well.”

“You do?”

“Sure. I’ve been there a few times.” Piper is surprised as she can’t remember seeing him in there. “The first tip I can give you is to stop giving your coffee away. You’re killing your business.” Piper’s mouth falls open at his words. He quickly corrects himself. “I’m sorry. I heard about the death of Ethel Bowers. I didn’t mean you’re killing your business literally.”

“It’s okay. I know what you meant, I think.” Piper tries to shake off the uneasy feeling she has.

“What I meant to say is, and what I should have said is, you don’t see me giving drinks away. I’d go bankrupt if I did.” The kitchen staff yells “Banks” louder than the first time. “It’s hard for me to work with him yelling at me at night.”

Piper laughs. She’s worked food service and knows what it’s like to try to talk to customers while doing your job at the same time. It’s also a must to deliver food as soon as it’s ready. No one likes cold food unless it’s a salad or fruit.

“I think you have hot food ready.”

“The story of my life. I always have hot food, but rarely do I get a hot dish.” He smiles and walks away.

Piper and Hannah watch as the server delivers food and entertains the other tables. “Mom, I think he was flirting with you.”

"He wasn't," Piper assures her. "He's like that with all of his tables."

Banks brings their food and they eat in silence. The fish and chips are flaky and delicious. As he said, this wouldn't be their only drink. They order another Bahama Mama in the middle of their dinner. *Smart business indeed*, Piper thinks to herself.

When they settle up their bill, Piper sees the name of the server on the bill. Carson.

"I noticed the kitchen staff calls you 'Banks,' but this says your name's Carson."

"I'm sorry. Now that things are slowing down, let me properly introduce myself." He wipes his hands off on a dishtowel tucked in back of his apron. "I'm Carson Eubanks. My friends and family call me Banks." He extends his hand and Piper takes it.

"You're Carson Eubanks, Junior?"

"That's right. You must have known my dad."

"No. I didn't know him. But I have heard of him. You've been in town all this time?"

"No. I'm just getting back actually. I've been back for only a few months."

"How long has your pub been opened?"

"Just a few weeks. Is this your first time coming here?"

"It is. It won't be our last. Everything was amazing, including the service."

"We aim to please."

Piper considers the timeline and he's been back in town for only a few months. Would he have any reason to kill Ethel? Piper doesn't know, but she's determined to find out.

CHAPTER 6

Piper drops off Hannah to get her car at work before she calls Lindsey.

"What's up?" Lindsey answers.

"I found Carson Eubanks."

There's a long pause.

"Okay. But he was never lost as he's at his final resting place at the cemetery."

"I mean his son."

"Oh. Did we know he had a son?"

"No, but we do now."

"Where are you?"

"I just dropped off Hannah at the sheriff's office to get her car. I'm heading home now."

"Good. I'll meet you there."

When Piper pulls in, Lindsey's sitting in the rocker on the front porch.

"Tell me everything," Lindsey says as Piper opens the car door.

"Can I get in the house first?"

"Can you move any faster?"

Once inside Piper makes some coffee and Lindsey sits at the kitchen table.

"Have you been to the new pub and eatery over on the river lately?"

"Yes. That's where Jace took me for our first date."

"You mean there's been more than one?"

"Maybe. What does the pub have to do with Carson Eubanks?"

"You're an investigative reporter and you don't know where I'm heading with this?"

Lindsey thinks for a moment. "What! Carson Eubanks is the owner of the pub."

"He is. And he's quite handsome *and* funny."

"How long has he been in town?"

"He said for a few months, but the pub's been opened only a few weeks."

Lindsey thinks that for a man to wait thirty years to kill the person he thinks is responsible for killing his father is brilliant. Who would suspect him after all this time? No one else would suspect him, would they? Well, Piper and Lindsey would, but who else?

"That's about the same time Ethel was killed."

"I already thought of that. But would he have reason to kill her?"

"Maybe if he felt she was responsible for his father's death."

"We need to talk to him and find out what brought him back here."

"Great idea. You do it."

Piper looks shocked. "Me? Why does it have to be me?"

"You've already met him so you have a rapport with him, and that means you're already one step closer to getting the truth than I am."

"But you're so much better at interacting with people than me."

"Interacting with or interrogating?"

"Same difference."

"Pfft. Just wear something low-cut and giggle a lot. He'll tell you everything you want to know plus some."

"Just because that works for you doesn't mean it works for everyone."

Lindsey stands and walks toward the kitchen door. "It works for all women. You just never tried it yet." She opens the door and leaves.

Lindsey's twenty years younger than Piper and she's pretty sure this may have worked for her twenty years ago; however, she doubts that to be true for her today.

~~~

The next morning, Piper takes Bailey out before heading to work. With Paul doing his three DUI days in jail, Piper's left to open, close, and run the coffeehouse by herself. She isn't excited about being solo, but this time without Paul will let her know just how much help he is.

She arrives at the coffeehouse earlier than usual to find Mildred sitting in the rocker crocheting.

"Have you been here all night?" Piper asks, confused as to why she's here so early.

"Heavens, no. I knew you were alone, so I thought I could keep you company." When Piper doesn't say anything, Mildred adds, "Or I could just wait right here for you to open."
~~~

Piper smiles and opens the door wide. "Don't be silly. Come on in, I'll start the coffee."

"Now that's an invitation I can't pass up."

"Good. I'll get your cart for you."

"Thank you, dear."

Piper places Mildred's cart close enough for her to reach it before she starts the coffee. "I wish I had some doughnuts to offer you while I make fresh, but I'm completely out."

Mildred starts to crochet. "It's okay. Your doughnuts are worth the wait."

"Thank you, Mildred. I appreciate that." Piper pushes the start button on the coffee pot. "I have to start making the doughnuts, so please help yourself to the coffee when it's done."

"I'll be fine. No need to worry about me."

"Mildred," Piper says.

"Yes, dear."

"I'm glad you're here with me this morning."

Mildred smiles. "I'm glad to be here, too."

Piper thinks that finally she and Mildred are becoming friends, and she couldn't be happier about that. It's hard being at odds with someone every day. It takes a lot of energy to dislike someone. This will surely make life a little easier.

Piper checks on Mildred as she pops in and out of the kitchen to and from the dining room while stocking the serving cabinet. Mildred stops crocheting and smiles whenever Piper enters the room. Although she's busy, she still takes the time to cater to Mildred by refilling her coffee, offering her another doughnut, and making small talk.

“I heard Ethel was at the library the night before she died.”

“I think she was there a lot. She and Harper were in a book club together.”

“Oh, I wasn’t aware of that.”

“Neither was I until Harper told me.”

“Who else was in this book club?”

“Just the two.”

“Doesn’t make much of a club, does it?”

“I guess not.”

When everything’s done, Piper opens the coffeehouse. The cleaning up will need to wait until closing time.

Lindsey comes in next and takes a seat at the counter before ordering a coffee with sugar and hazelnut creamer, and a glazed doughnut.

“Hey, Mildred,” Lindsey says.

“Lindsey,” Mildred says, looking over her glasses.

“How are you doing this fine morning?”

“Not as good as you.”

Piper looks surprised but not as surprised as Lindsey does at Mildred’s comment. “What’s that supposed to mean?”

“I heard you were entertaining *all night* last night.”

“Mildred,” Lindsey huffs. “You can’t believe everything you hear.”

Mildred pushes her glasses up further on her nose and starts to crochet again. “I know and hear a lot more than I get credit for.”

Piper and Lindsey look at each other again. For some reason this sounds like a statement with a double meaning. Does Mildred know something about Ethel’s murder? Is that what she’s talking about or is it strictly pertaining to Lindsey and her male companion?

Lindsey eats her doughnut quickly and takes the rest of her coffee to go with her. Piper suspects Mildred’s embarrassed her enough to make her leave.

“I’ll meet you at Ethel’s after work.”

“Okay. Do you want to go sooner and I’ll meet you there when I get off?” Piper asks.

“No. We’ll go in together.”

Mildred looks over her glasses at Lindsey and shakes her head. “You’re not scared, are you, Lindsey?”

“No,” she lies. “I just don’t want to go in without Piper.”

“It’s not the dead you have to be afraid of.”

If Lindsey didn’t know better, she might think this was a threat. The door opens and Piper immediately smiles. Lindsey and Mildred both stare at the man walking into the coffeehouse.

“Good morning, Ma’am,” he says with a nod of his head as he passes Mildred.

“Sonny,” Mildred replies.

He walks up to the counter and looks over at Lindsey and smiles a friendly smile. “Hi.”

Lindsey clears her throat. “Hello,” she says seductively.

The man looks away and focuses his attention on Piper. His smile is larger this time as if he’s seeing a longtime friend. “Hello, stranger.”

“Didn’t expect to see you so soon.”

“I was in the neighborhood.”

Piper nervously adjusts her apron. “Is that right?”

“It is.”

Lindsey sits back down and decides she’s in no hurry to leave after all. She coughs, catching Banks’ attention.

Despite being several years younger than the man, Lindsey offers her hand. “Hi, I’m Lindsey Miles. I’m a reporter for the local newspaper.”

The man gently takes her hand. “Hi. I’m Banks, owner/operator of The pub on the River.”

Lindsey darts a quick look at Piper. “Oh. You’re the new owner of the new pub. What’s the name of your pub?”

“That is the name. The pub on the River.”

Mildred snorts a laugh.

“Oh,” Lindsey shakes his hand and smiles. “It’s nice to meet you.”

Mildred tosses her handkerchief on the floor away from her. “Lindsey, would you be a dear and get that for me?” When Lindsey hands it to Mildred, Mildred whispers, “Why not just toss your bloomers at him?” Lindsey cringes at the mention of bloomers. She likes to refer to her undergarments as intimates. Bloomers sound like granny panties and what Lindsey wears is far from granny panties.

Her eyes get big as she can't believe what's coming out of Mildred's mouth this morning. "For God's sake, he's old enough to be your father."

Lindsey knows she's right, but a little flirting never hurt anyone. Lindsey stands and watches as Piper bats her eyes and does her own flirting with the newcomer. She can't remember a time when Piper seemed interested in any man. She walks up to the counter, gets her purse and coffee, and bids farewell before leaving.

"So, do you live around here?" Piper asks Banks.

"No, not really. But I woke up with this craving for coffee and doughnuts."

"What can I get for you?" Piper feels someone staring at her and chances a glance at Mildred, who's watching them both over her glasses. Piper quickly looks away.

The door opens and in walk two more customers.

"I'll take a glazed doughnut and a coffee to go."

Piper greets her new customers before getting Banks' order. She hands it to him and rings it up.

"Thank you and come again."

"I will. Thank you." She watches as he nods to Mildred before leaving.

~~~

At the end of the day Piper realizes just how much help Paul is in the coffeehouse. Although Piper opened and closed in a timely manner, it's much easier with Paul here assisting.

Piper rushes home to take Bailey out before heading over to Ethel's house. Ethel's sister, Abigail, should be here to go
~~~

through the house in a few days. Not everything will be inventoried, but hopefully most of it will be done.

Before heading to Ethel's, Piper stops by the jewelers to get Ethel's jewelry appraised.

"I can tell you one thing, everything here is real gold."

"What about the stones?" Piper asks.

He looks through his jeweler's loupe — non-jewelers call it a magnifying glass — and carefully inspects the stones set in each piece. "They're also real." He sets the loupe down. "It'll take me a few days to get you an estimate on it all. I can also clean it and tighten the stones for you."

"That would be great. Thank you."

"No problem."

"If you can, I need them back before I can auction off Ethel Bowers' estate."

"These belong to Ethel?"

"Yes, that's right. Why?"

"I had no idea she owned such valuable vintage pieces."

"Neither did I."

"I guess we didn't know her as well as we thought." He places the jewelry into a lock box and hands Piper a receipt for the jewelry.

"When are you planning her estate sale?"

"Next Sunday."

"I'll call you in a few days."

"Thank you."

Piper leaves and calls the sheriff's office for an escort before pulling up at Ethel's house.

Lindsey's standing outside of the police cruiser talking to Jace.

She gets out of the car and they walk up to the door together. Piper makes sure it's locked before doing anything else. They both look relieved when the door's secured shut, as it should be.

"I'll be glad when this is over and done with."

Piper get goosebumps on the nape of her neck. "Me, too."

"Stay here while I check inside."

"Thanks, Jace," Lindsey purrs.

"I'll just be a minute."

Once he's inside, Piper asks, "Does he need to do that since the door was locked?"

"I guess so. I'd feel better if he did."

Once it's clear, he kisses Lindsey and leaves.

"Why don't you start taking all of the family pictures off of the wall and stacking the smaller ones on the table and then stack the larger pictures along the wall?"

"What are you going to do?"

"I'm going to finish the kitchen."

"Okay."

Piper's beginning to think Lindsey's either scared of ghosts or she's afraid the possible intruder might come back.

Piper works hard at cleaning the kitchen as there isn't a lot to inventory. She places the pots and pans in boxes and sets them off to the side. There's a few antique-looking teapots and serving dishes that Piper's sure these are things Abigail would like to keep of her sister's.

She's excited to see how much they got done at Ethel's house today. She's hoping by Monday she'll be able to meet with Abigail, have the appraisals back on the jewelry, and list the house and the contents with a local auction company for Sunday.

"Where are you heading now?"

Piper locks up and they walk outside together. "I was going to have some dinner. Do you want to join me?"

"Sure," Lindsey says. "I'll drive."

A few minutes later Lindsey pulls up at the pub that Banks owns. Piper shouldn't be surprised but she is.

"What are you doing here?"

"We're here to get some information from Banks."

"He'll be too busy to talk," Piper says, getting out of the car.

"I doubt that. Once he sees you, I'm sure he'll make time."

Piper rolls her eyes. "I'm not like you. Guys don't rush over to talk with me."

"We'll see."

They walk into the pub and see that Banks is standing at the hostess station talking with an employee. It looks like he may be fully staffed this evening.

"Table for two?" the hostess asks.

"Yes, we'd like to sit outside if you have something open."

Banks looks at Piper as if he doesn't see Lindsey standing there with her. "I'll seat her, Amy."

"There's two of them, Banks," Amy whispers.

"Of course there are." He looks at Lindsey and then Piper. "Follow me, ladies."

He walks them through the pub to the waterside dining area. "We really need to stop meeting like this," he whispers. Lindsey smiles and Piper fidgets as if she's uncomfortable by his insinuation that this is a planned meeting. It's been years since Piper's divorce and she hasn't dated since. But she still feels like Banks' comment is a bit flirty. He doesn't apologize for making Piper uncomfortable. It's almost like he's enjoying it. "Best seat in the house," he says as he pulls out a chair for Piper and then one for Lindsey.

"Thank you." Lindsey looks around the patio at the other diners and then at the river. "I can see why."

"It's beautiful. Thank you."

"You're welcome. I'll send your server right over."

Banks walks away and Piper and Lindsey watch as he walks into the darkened pub. They're both surprised when they see Mildred sitting at a table. They didn't see her when they walked in. Banks hands her a to-go container of food and a carryout cup possibly filled with hot coffee. Then he walks her outside as she pulls her cart behind her.

"She does get around," Lindsey says as she looks away from Mildred.

Piper wasn't sure exactly sure how Lindsey meant it, but she replies anyway. "That she does."

They order drinks and dinner before Banks returns to their table. “May I?” he asks with his hand on an extra chair.

“Please.” Lindsey knew he would return but wondered what took him so long.

Lindsey picks up her frosted beer mug and sucks in the foam. She knows it is a sensual move and she likes to see men’s reaction to it. However, she’s disappointed when Banks doesn’t notice.

“May I assume you liked the food enough to come back again?”

Piper refolds her napkin. “The food was delicious.”

Lindsey wastes no time in questioning Banks. “So, tell us something about yourself, Banks.”

“What do you want to know?”

“How long have you been in town?”

“I’ve been back a few months but just recently opened the pub.”

“Oh, you lived here before?” Lindsey already knows that he lived in Pineapple Grove while his father was alive. Working at the newspaper allows Lindsey access to old newspaper articles and other things. Since she found out Carson Eubanks had a son, she’s been searching for any news pertaining to him.

“That’s right. I left right after my father was murdered.”

“I’m sorry,” Piper says, genuinely sad for him.

“Thank you. It was a long time ago.”

Lindsey leans into the table. “Who was your father?”

“Carson Eubanks. You wouldn’t have known him.”

"Then you must have known Ethel Bowers?"

Piper's surprised that Lindsey is wasting no time asking Banks questions.

"I did. My father died the night before he was to marry her."

"Did they ever find out who killed your father?"

"Sadly, no, they never did."

"Were there any suspects?"

"There were several. Ethel was one, but no one was charged." Banks stays focused on Lindsey. "What's up with all the questions?"

"Nothing," Lindsey lies. "Have you heard that Ethel Bowers was recently killed?"

"I did hear that. She died the same way my father was killed."

"Did you suspect Ethel of killing your father?"

Banks leans back in his chair and runs his hand through his hair. "It doesn't matter now what I thought."

Lindsey looks over at Piper. The investigative reporter in Lindsey is taking over. Piper hopes she doesn't regret being so forward.

"Did you come back here to kill Ethel?"

Piper spills her drink, but no one at the table seems to notice.

"No, I liked Ethel. I even have a key to her house."

"You have a key to Ethel's duplex?" Piper asks.

"That's right."

"Why would *you* have a key?"

"When I moved back in town, I stopped by to say hello. She offered to let me stay in the empty half of her duplex until I got my own place. I stayed for a while until I closed on this pub, then I moved into the upstairs apartment here. When she gave me the key, she told me that she had the same type of locks on her door, and my key would work for her half of the duplex if I ever needed anything."

"Why would she offer to let you stay with her?" Lindsey asks.

"I know she didn't get along with most people in this town, but at one point she was going to be my stepmother. I never knew my mother when I was growing up so she was the closest thing to a mom that I had. I tried to return the key after I moved out, but she told me to hold on to it."

"Oh, I'm sorry," Lindsey says. "I didn't mean to pry."

"I think you did." Banks smiles.

"You're right, I did. But I didn't mean to seem so heartless."

"It's okay. I can understand how it may have looked. You have to know that Ethel was near and dear to my heart. I would have never wanted anything like this to happen to her." He inhales deeply, "But to answer your earlier question, I came back to Pineapple Grove to find out who killed my father. It's just a coincidence that Ether Bowers was killed upon my return. I had no reason to kill her." The server brings their food and everyone remains quiet until she leaves. "Why does this sound like an interrogation? I thought you said this morning you were a newspaper reporter? Are you looking to write an article for the newspaper?"

“No, not at all.”

“Then what’s up with all the questions?”

Lindsey decides to be truthful as she feels he’s been truthful with her. “We’re searching to find out who killed Ethel.” Banks looks over at Piper. “That’s when we discovered the cold case file on your father.”

“Do you work for the police department?” Lindsey shakes her head. “Do you have experience in crime solving?”

“I am an investigative reporter.”

“I mean no offense by my next comment,” he says.

“None taken. Yet.”

“But…you’re a reporter in Pineapple Grove. Nothing ever happens here.”

“I hate to point out the obvious, but there have been two unsolved murders.”

“Two points taken, but why are you taking it upon yourselves to solve them? Why not let the police handle this?”

“You mean like they solved your father’s murder.”

“A third point taken.”

Piper leans into the table. “Ethel died in back of my coffeehouse. There’s rumors going around that I could have been responsible. I’d like to clear my name *and* reputation before they’re completely ruined.”

Banks watches Piper. She has dark circles under her eyes that he didn’t notice earlier. However, they don’t take away from her beauty.

“I’m in.”

"Wait? What?"

He readjusts his seat so he's looking directly at Piper. "I want to help clear your name, and I also want to know who killed my father."

Lindsey asks, "You don't mind sharing some things about your father's murder with us, do you?"

"Not if it'll help find his murderer and clear Piper's name."

"Great! We'll be in touch."

~~~

Over the next few days, Piper and Lindsey finish the inventory of Ethel's house and then Piper arranges to have the house and the contents auctioned off with a local auction house on Sunday. Piper and Lindsey work hard to make the house presentable for sale. They place all of the family photos out on the dining room table along with some of Ethel's personal items. Paul takes some used items and donates them to a local domestic violence shelter, he takes several boxes of books and gives them to Harper at the library, and then he takes the rest of the boxes of canned foods and donates them to the local food bank. Finally, everything is ready.

The jewelers call with a dollar amount for the value of the vintage jewelry that Ethel owned. Piper asks the jewelers if they could hold on to the jewelry for a bit longer. Piper thinks the items are safer in the jewelry store than anywhere else.

Before leaving Ethel's house, she calls Abigail to confirm her arrival tomorrow.

"Abigail, this is Piper Armstrong. How are you?"
~~~

“Hi, dear. I’m sorry to say I’m not doing well this evening.”

“Oh, I’m sorry to hear that.”

“Don’t be. It’s all in the process of aging that many are denied.”

Such simple words but so meaningful.

“I was just calling to see if you are still planning on coming to Pineapple Grove in the morning.”

“I meant to call you. Sadly, I’m not able to make it tomorrow.”

Piper can hear the disappointment in her voice. “It’s okay. You don’t need to be here. The auction is planned for Sunday. Is that okay with you?”

“That was fast.” Piper takes that as a compliment. It was a lot of work for her, Lindsey, and Paul to do in preparation for the auction. “I can be there on Saturday, then maybe I can stay for the auction on Sunday. I just can’t make it tomorrow like I planned.”

“Okay. I put some things off to the side that I thought you’d like, but I’m not sure about Ethel’s clothing, shoes, and things like that.”

“To be honest I have everything I need and I don’t have room to store unnecessary things.”

“I understand. I can donate her clothing to a local thrift shop if that’ll be all right.”

“She would like that.”

“There’s one more thing.”

“Yes, dear.”

“The jewelry I found. I finally got an appraisal on it.”

“Don’t tell me the amount. I’m not ready to die of a heart attack.” Piper stops herself from chuckling. “Can you just tell me if one of the items was an engagement ring?”

“As a matter of fact, there was a solitaire diamond ring along with some other pieces.”

“We should give it back to Carson Eubanks.”

Piper understood that Abigail knew Carson was dead. Does she have dementia? “I thought you knew that Carson Eubanks passed away, Abigail.”

“I know Carson senior was killed, but he had a son with the same name.” She sounds like she’s getting winded. “Maybe you can find the son and give him back his father’s ring. Maybe it’ll have some sentimental value to him.”

Piper cuts the call short as it sounds like Abigail needs to rest.

“I’ll see what I can do and with the other stuff, I’ll use my best judgment.”

“Thank you, dear.”

“Goodbye, Abigail.”

“Goodbye, Piper.”

~~~

The next morning, Piper and Paul pull up to the coffeehouse. A police cruiser rides by and Paul and Piper offer a friendly wave. Piper’s happy to see Mildred sitting in the rocking chair on the front porch.

As Piper makes her way to the front porch, Mildred’s fast asleep with her afghan spread across her lap. *Must be nice*
~~~

to be able to sleep anywhere, Piper thinks to herself. She unlocks the door and places her things on the closet table while Paul wakes Mildred and brings her and her cart inside.

Since Paul's back from jail, Piper has time to speak with Mildred alone. Piper makes the coffee while Paul starts in the kitchen. When the coffee's done, Piper sits down beside Mildred.

"How are you, Mildred?"

"I'm pretty good for an old lady." Mildred watches Piper. "What's on your mind, Piper?"

"I've been thinking about Ethel and how tragic her death's been."

"She sure is stirring up some gossip."

"That she is. Have you happened to have heard anything?"

Mildred begins to crochet. "I hear lots of things."

"About Ethel?"

Mildred doesn't make eye contact. "About Ethel and others in Pineapple Grove."

"Have you heard who killed her?"

"Can't say I heard that."

"Would you tell me if you had heard something?"

"Can't say I would."

~~~

Hunter makes his way back to the nursing home that his mother is staying in. Today's not a planned trip, but after
~~~

she called him and told him about Piper stopping by she insisted that he come to her so they can talk in person.

“I recently had a visitor.”

“You have visitors a lot of days.”

“But I didn’t know this one.”

“Who was it?”

“She said she owned the coffeehouse here in town.”

“What did she want?”

“She was asking about Carson Eubanks.”

“What did you tell her?”

“I sounded like a senile old coot. I had her so confused when she left here she probably didn’t believe anything I had to say.” Ruby adjusts her lap blanket. “Did you get the item out of Ethel’s house like I asked you?”

“I did.”

“You sure they didn’t see you coming or going?”

“I’m positive. No one was around.”

“I’m glad it worked out. Maybe they won’t know anyone was in there.”

“They didn’t see me, but there’s something else you need to know.” Ruby glares at her son. He continues, “While I was there, my shirt sleeve got caught on the kitchen drawer pull handle and I lost a button off my shirt. I didn’t notice the missing button until I made it back home.”

“Oh, Hunter. You just can’t seem to do anything right. Get rid of the item and get rid of the shirt. I don’t want anyone to be able to place you at Ethel’s.”

"I disposed of the item already. It can't be traced."

"Okay, good. Now get rid of the shirt."

"It's as good as gone."

Ruby seems to relax.

"Don't forget, everyone will be here Saturday to pick me up for dinner. Make sure you're ready at four o'clock."

"I'll meet everyone here like I do every Saturday."

CHAPTER 7

On Friday evening Piper gets a call from Banks asking her to meet him at his pub. She changes from her tee shirt into a white blouse and drives the short distance to his pub. When she gets there, she takes a seat at the bar and waits for him. He walks up to her and smiles.

"You look great."

"Thank you." She blushes, then ignores the compliment. "What's up?"

"I have someone here you might want to talk to." Piper looks around the crowded pub. "Do you see that man sitting in that last booth against the wall?"

Piper looks over Banks' shoulder and sees the back of an older man's head. His hair is gray and thinning, almost bald on the top back part of his head.

"Yeah, I see him. I don't think I know who he is as I can't see his face, though."

"He came in about forty-five minutes ago. I was working, but I got the feeling that someone was watching me. I looked around the place and noticed that he was looking at me. I thought something may have been wrong with his food or service and he wanted to speak with a manager, so I went over to his table to check on him." Banks inhales deeply. "He immediately apologized for staring, but he said that he couldn't help notice that I look familiar. Before I could get a word out, he asked me if I was Carson Eubanks' son. He said I look just like him. I told him that I am and he told me his name."

Piper's hoping this story gets interesting soon. "And who is he?"

"His name's Maverick Smoker."

“The owner of the pub where your dad died?”

“The same. He apologized and said he’s always felt responsible for my father’s murder.”

“Why? Did he kill him?”

Banks looks back at Maverick Smoker, who’s still sitting in the booth. “I don’t think so.”

“I told him another person recently died from the same kind of poison that killed my father. He told me he knew about the new murder and he’s known Ethel for nearly his whole life. He asked me if I suspected that the two murders were linked.”

“I wonder if he knows something?”

“I told him I had a friend who was following the two murders closely and she might like to speak with him if he had a few extra minutes. He said to call you and he’d be happy to talk with you.”

“Well, what are we waiting on? Let’s go meet Mr. Smoker.”

They both walk over to the booth and Banks introduces Piper.

“Mr. Smoker, this is the woman I was telling you about, Piper Armstrong, my… um, friend.”

Piper looks at Banks. Was he about to introduce himself as more than a friend? Piper doesn’t mind the thought of it, but it is a little early to call it anything more than a friendship. She extends her hand and Maverick gently shakes it before the two settle into the booth across from him.

“Hello, Mr. Smoker.”

"Please call me Maverick."

"Maverick," Piper begins again. "I'm not sure how familiar you are with the residents of Pineapple Grove, but a woman was recently found dead behind my coffeehouse."

"I owned a pub here some time ago so I'm familiar with my generation. I don't know the younger ones, but I knew right away who this fellow's father was."

"Can you tell me anything about Carson Eubanks' murder?"

"I'm not sure how much help I can be. I don't know who killed Carson. If I did, believe me, I would have told the police a long time ago."

"I didn't figure you knew who killed him. I was just hoping you could tell me more about the people who were there that night. I've spoken with a few people who were around back then. I know Stephanie Guest was there. I thought it was odd that she was there, then she bought the place and turned it into an inn."

"You think Stephanie killed Carson Eubanks?"

"I don't. But some of the people I spoke with said she was a suspect."

"I can see some things in Pineapple Grove never change."

Piper looks at Banks.

"What do you mean?"

"Gossip. No one can mind their own business. I always thought this place should be called Gossip Grove."

Piper hides her laugh.

"Are you saying Stephanie Guest was never a suspect?"

“I’m just saying I don’t think Stephanie is capable of killing anyone.”

“Why did she buy the inn so quickly after Carson was killed?”

“It was a good location and she got it at a great price.”

“Why did you sell it?”

“Are you kidding?” Piper shakes her head. He continues, “I was a married man. Once Carson was murdered, my wife insisted I sell the pub. I had already made enough money from the place and I figured nobody would want to come back and drink there because they were afraid of getting poisoned. So, I sold it almost immediately and Miss Guest bought it.” He looks over at Banks. “I think she saw an opportunity to make an investment and she wisely jumped on it.”

“I see.” Piper wishes Lindsey was here since Lindsey is better at interrogating than she is.

“I had another personal reason to want to leave as well. I think everything worked out for me the way it was supposed to. I’m really impressed with what Stephanie did with the place.”

“Is that where you’re staying? At the inn?”

“It is. She was nice enough not to charge me for the room. I always liked Stephanie and I’m glad she made good use of the place.” He takes a sip of his beer. “I didn’t even know it was the same place.”

“Do you mind if I ask what the personal reason was that you had to want to leave?”

“That’s where I have to draw the line. Like I said the reason is personal.”

"I understand. I apologize for asking." Piper looks over at Banks before looking back at the elderly man. "Can you recall if a woman named Ruby Gallagher was at the pub the night Carson Eubanks was killed?"

"What was that?" he says, cupping his hand over his ear.

Piper repeats it again for Maverick.

"Gallagher? The name sounds familiar, but I can't seem to place it. It was so many years ago."

"She's the one who told my friend and me about Carson senior. Well, she didn't exactly tell us. She told her son and he told my friend, who then told me after my friend confirmed it was true from the old newspaper."

"It's making my head spin. As I said, I always thought this place should be called Gossip Grove. Where did your 'unnamed friend' find a newspaper that old to look through?" He makes air quotes like it's some big secret or something. Maybe it is for all he knows

"Well, she's a reporter for the local paper. They keep a copy of every newspaper they ever printed."

"I best be getting back to the inn. My wife will be wondering where I am. If I can remember anything about that Gallagher woman, I'll get back in touch with Banks."

"Thank you for your help, Mr. Smoker."

"Call me Maverick, please," he says as he puts his hat on his head and stands to leave.

Piper thanks Banks and leaves.

On her way home, Piper finishes up some last-minute things she needs to do for the auction on Sunday morning. She calls the jewelers to let them know she's on her way to pick up Ethel's jewelry.

~~~

On Saturday, Paul and Piper close the coffeehouse. They need to take care of everything for the auction on Sunday.

Lindsey meets Piper at Ethel's house to meet with the auctioneer. He needs to get the house appraised and he wants to look over the merchandise.

"Everything looks good, but I think we should plan on having the auction outside tomorrow."

"Oh," Piper says.

"Ethel has a lot of stuff and there's no way we'll be able to get everyone in this crowded space."

"I see."

"Trust me when I tell you you'll double your money by doing it this way."

Piper trusted him, but she wasn't thrilled about having to move everything down the stairs and outside.

"She has a lot of stuff to move."

"If you have someone who can move the furniture into the garage today, I'll have my guys move everything else tomorrow during the auction."

"Okay. I can get someone to do that."

"Good. I'll see you tomorrow bright and early."

Paul and Scott are able to move some of the furniture into the two-car garage and what didn't fit, they left it on the first floor of the duplex, while his mom and Lindsey straighten up the inside and wait for Abigail to show up. Piper knows Abigail isn't feeling well and she doesn't want to call her to see if she is still coming. If she comes, great;
~~~

if she doesn't come, Piper will have to use her best judgment about Ethel's personal items.

While waiting for Abigail to arrive and supervising her son and his friend, Piper and Lindsey talk about Banks.

Lindsey says, "So what do you think about Banks having a key to this place?"

"I don't know," answers Piper. "His story seems believable. Ethel was the person whom his father was going to marry. And besides that, he is very handsome and let's not forget funny. Maybe I just want to believe him."

"I just don't like the idea that Ethel's coffee could have been poisoned in her own home and he has a key to the place. Then to top it off someone was here when we showed up a couple weeks ago. There were no signs of forced entry and I, for one, think the perpetrator had to have a key."

"Or we could have forgotten to lock up. Sheriff Abbott and his guys were here as well. They could have left the place unlocked. But that doesn't explain how they could have gotten in while Ethel was still alive. Surely, she would have noticed that someone was in her duplex, unless they had a key."

"How long ago do you think Banks moved out?"

"He said he moved out when he closed on the pub and the pub's been opened for a month or more." Piper looks around the house. "Two months maybe. I don't think Banks is our guy." Piper looks at her chipped nail polish. "I forgot to tell you that he called me last night."

"He, who? Banks?"

"He wanted me to come over to his pub. When I got there, I was shocked to find out why he called. Maverick Smoker was in town and he was in his pub."

"And?"

"Banks asked him if he would be willing to talk with me about the night Carson was killed. Sadly, he didn't have any useful information to offer. I asked him about Stephanie Guest. He didn't think she was capable of murder. He said he wanted to sell the pub quickly after Carson was poisoned and Stephanie wanted it as an investment. He did say, however, that he had a personal reason to want to leave town."

"What was that?"

"He wouldn't tell me. He said that's where he'd have to draw the line. I asked him about Ruby Gallagher as well. He didn't seem to remember her. He did say the last name sounded familiar, but he couldn't place it. If he remembers her, he's going to get back in touch with Banks."

"On a day that someone gets murdered in your pub you don't remember who all was there? That doesn't sound right." Lindsey thinks about how long ago it's been and Maverick Smoker's current age. "I guess it was a long time ago."

"It was a very long time ago."

Lindsey leans forward in the chair. "Speaking of the Gallaghers, I ran into Hunter the other day when I was dropping off Ethel's clothing at the consignment shop.

"What was Hunter doing there?"

"Donating some clothes. It didn't look like he had much. A few funky shirts that he always wears. I guess every little bit helps."

“Yeah, every little bit does, but why make the trip to drop off a few items? Why not put it up and when you have a bag full bring it all at once?” Piper remembers the button that she found on the kitchen floor. “Were any of the shirts orange?”

“I don’t know. I didn’t look that closely. They were all kinds of funky looking colors.”

Piper asks, “Do you remember that button we found in the kitchen?”

“That funky orange color?”

“That’s the one.”

“Do you think any his funky shirts had funky-looking buttons?”

Lindsey smiles. “I think it’s a great possibility.”

“Can you go back to the store and see if they have any of the shirts out for sale yet? If they do, buy them and bring them back here. I want to try and match the shirt buttons to the button we found. If it matches, Hunter may be a person of interest.”

“But he couldn’t have been responsible for what happened thirty years ago.”

“True, but maybe he knows something. Maybe Ruby knows more than she’s saying?”

Lindsey rushes out the door and Piper gets the button she found the other day from the kitchen drawer and waits for Lindsey to get back. In the meantime, she searches through the box of jewelry she got from the jewelers until she finds the engagement ring that Banks’ dad gave to Ethel. All of the jewelry has a price tag on it and Piper is surprised to see that the ring is valued at nearly five thousand dollars. Piper calls Banks and asks him to come over to Ethel's to help her until Lindsey makes it back. Piper also wants to give Banks back the ring his father gave to Ethel all those years ago.

While she waits for Banks and Lindsey, Piper tries to help Paul and Scott but soon she realizes she's only in the way.

There's a knock at the door and she wonders why Banks didn't just use the key he said Ethel gave him.

"Hey, thanks for coming over on such short notice."

"No thanks needed. What can I help you with?"

Piper hands Banks the engagement ring. "First, I want to give you this."

"Proposing so soon?" Banks teases.

Piper blushes and looks away so he can't see her. "Does it look familiar?"

The first thing he does is look at the price tag. "Whew! Nice piece." He closely inspects the ring. "Am I supposed to have seen this ring before?"

"Perhaps not." He attempts to hand the ring back to Piper, but she doesn't take it. "I spoke with Ethel's sister, Abigail, and she insisted that we give this ring back to you. I believe it's the ring your father gave to Ethel when he proposed."

He looks at the ring more closely. "Dad had great taste."

"I thought so. I had Ethel's jewelry cleaned and appraised by a local jeweler. The price tag is what he's appraised the ring to be worth in today's market."

"Thank you for doing that and please thank Abigail for me for returning it. She didn't need to do that, but it's greatly appreciated."

"You're welcome and I'll be sure to thank her."

Banks looks at the ring more closely. "Who knows, maybe one day I'll find someone to give it to."

Lindsey knocks before entering Ethel's duplex. She finds Banks and Piper straightening up the house for the big auction.

"I have the shirts that Hunter donated and you're right, one of them is missing a button."

"Are you sure these are Hunter's?"

"Ashley was working. I asked her if Hunter donated some items and if he did, I needed them. Of course, she wanted to know why."

"What did you tell her?"

"I told her his mother was having a birthday and I wanted to make her something special out of his clothing for her."

"You're good."

"Thank you. She said she didn't have time to price them and put them on the rack yet."

"I told her I would take them, as is. She went into the back room and brought out these beauties."

Piper and Banks make a face before Piper grabs the orange and green shirt and rushes into the dining room to match it with the button from the drawer.

"What's going on with this shirt?" Banks asks.

"We think we know who killed Ethel."

"And you're just now telling me?"

“We don’t know for sure yet. Plus, we’ve been wrong before.”

Piper takes the button and holds it up to the buttons on the shirt. “It’s a match.” Piper says, “I didn’t really expect to find a match. I’m not sure what to do now.”

“I just talked to Jace. He should be here any minute.”

Banks asks, “Who’s Jace?”

Piper looks at Banks. “He’s a deputy that Lindsey’s been seeing.”

“And who’s Hunter?”

“Lindsey’s photographer at the newspaper.”

“So, it was your photographer that you think is linked to the murder of Ethel?”

“Let’s just say he’s a person of interest.”

“His mom said she was at Maverick’s pub the night your father was killed.”

“Who’s his mom?”

“Ruby Gallagher.”

“She’s the one you asked Maverick about but he couldn’t remember her, right?”

“Yes, but he either didn’t know the name…”

“Or her name changed,” Lindsey interrupts.

“You work for the paper. Wouldn’t they have printed something about her getting married?”

“They probably would have, but I would have to go through an incredible number of wedding announcements in the newspapers to find the one I was looking for. I'd be dead by the time I found it."

"I'm going back over there," Piper says.

"Over where?" Lindsey asks.

"To talk with Ruby. She knows something and I need to find out how Hunter's button got into Ethel's house."

"Hunter once told me while we were working together that his family has dinner every Saturday evening with his mom and as many family members who can make it," Lindsey says.

"At the nursing home?"

"No. Some meet up at the nursing home while others get a table at the restaurant and wait there for them to arrive."

"What time is that?"

"I can't really remember. Five o'clock, maybe."

Piper looks at her watch. "It's four-thirty now."

"Maybe it'll work out better if her room's empty. That way you can look around before confronting her."

"Good idea."

"I'll go with you," Banks insists.

"No, it'll be better if I go by myself. I've already been there once so it won't look suspicious if I show up again. If we both get caught looking around, they may suspect something and throw us both out."

Banks doesn't agree or disagree. He's sure Piper's already made up her mind and nothing's going to change that.

"I'll drive and wait in the car while you go in. I'm not going to be that far away if things go wrong." Banks doesn't give her an option. It's a statement, not a question.

"Okay, that might be a good idea. Let's hurry up and get out of here before Jace comes and tries to stop me. Lindsey, you stay here until he comes. Keep an eye out for Ethel's sister as well. She could show up at some point today. Tell Jace what's going on, but don't tell him that we went over to Ruby's."

"What do I tell him?"

"I don't know, you're a reporter. Make something up."

Banks and Piper look at each other, wondering if her statement will offend Lindsey.

"Okay, I can do that."

No offense must have been taken.

"Oh, one more thing."

Lindsey looks up at Piper. "What's that?"

"Ethel's sister may show up today. Let her look through the house, and give her the pictures, the jewelry box, and the box of antiques I set off to the side for her if I'm not back."

"Will do. Be careful."

~~~

Piper and Banks drive to the nursing home. Banks parks as far away from the entrance as he can while still having a visual of the front door. He wants to make sure he can see who comes and goes.

"Maybe it is a good idea that you came."
~~~

Banks already knows it was a good idea, but he asks anyway, "Why is that?"

"Well, we don't know if they left yet. You can go in and act like you're looking for someone and see if her room's empty. If they see me, they'll be suspicious."

"Okay, that's another good point."

Banks gets the room number from Piper and makes his way into the nursing home. When he finds Ruby's room, he sees at least ten people waiting outside. Probably more are in the room.

I hope she didn't die, Banks thinks to himself. *Maybe she was murdered, too. If she was, then we're back to the beginning. No suspects and another murder to solve. But what would the chances be Ruby was also murdered? Slim to none, I hope.*

He doesn't wait around to see what's going on as he doesn't want to be seen by anyone. If Maverick Smoker thinks Banks looks like his father, maybe others in town who remember him will, too. He hurries back outside to tell Piper.

"I think she's dead. There's a dozen people standing outside her room in the hallway."

Piper turns in her seat so she can face Banks. "You're kidding?"

"No. The hallways packed with people waiting near her room."

"Did they look sad?"

"Sad? No, not really. They all seemed to be having a good time."

Piper gives him an eye roll. "Then I doubt that she died."

"I don't know. I know some people who'd be mighty glad if a few of the residents of Pineapple Grove keeled over."

Piper thinks she knows a few, too.

"They all must have met up here at the nursing home instead of the restaurant for dinner."

Piper looks over at him. "I doubt that. Some probably meet here and some are probably at the restaurant getting a table big enough for everyone."

Banks adds, "Okay, that's probably more accurate than they're here for her death."

Piper looks over at Banks. "You were kidding about thinking she was dead, right?"

"I was."

"I thought so." After Piper and Banks wait there for almost ten minutes, a large group of people walk outside. Ruby is nearly the last to exit in her wheelchair, which is being pushed by a middle-aged man. "That's Ruby in the wheelchair."

Piper watches as they walk to their cars.

"Do you know anyone?" Piper asks Banks.

"Can't say I do."

"Me either."

"Let me guess. The one wearing the bright green shirt is Lindsey's photographer, Hunter."

"That's him."

"He's easy to spot."

Piper looks over but doesn't say anything although she agrees with Banks. Hunter's shirt is very easy to see in a crowd.

After the group of people drives off, Piper nonchalantly walks inside the nursing home while Banks waits in the car. Once she gets in the room, she starts looking for anything she can find linking Ruby or Hunter to Ethel or to Carson. She picks up the calendar everyone uses to sign in on. Every Saturday on the calendar, the date is covered with as many names as will fit in the small space. She sees names like Ed, Mike, Beth, Sally, and Hunter. Piper looks over all the names, then flips back to the previous months to make sure nobody out of the normal people came to see her around the time of Ethel's death. No names stick out from the normal Saturday visitors. Piper thinks of how blessed Ruby is to have so many people who care for her enough to come visit. She knows some people in nursing homes never get visitors. Not noticing anything suspicious, Piper places the calendar back on the wall and continues to look around the room. All that's here are several family pictures, a few cards, Ruby's clothes, and some old movies and books. On her bedside table are a couple bags of those orange candy peanuts and a pitcher of ice water. Piper picks up the bag of candy peanuts and laughs at a memory. She remembers her own granddad eating these decades ago. It was the one candy her grandparents could keep in the house that the grandkids wouldn't eat.

Feeling like she's hit another dead end, Piper leaves the room and heads back out to Banks' waiting car.

Banks studies her face as she buckles herself into the seat. "By the look on your face, I'm guessing you came up empty handed."

"It was a waste of time. I was hoping she would have something lying around that would be of help. I guess when people move into a nursing home they don't bring much with them."

"They just have a small space to keep items they use daily. A few articles of clothing, some hygiene items, and a few pictures. Maybe some books."

The drive back to Ethel's is a quiet one. Piper hates to admit this might be another cold case murder. Other than the button that came off of Hunter's shirt, there's no other clues as to who poisoned Ethel. The button could have been in the house for days before Piper found it. Maybe Hunter lost a button while he was here visiting Ethel. That's possible, but Ethel kept an impeccably clean house. If there were a button laying in the middle of the floor, she's certain Ethel would have saw it and picked it up. Another question is, who left the door open?

When Piper finds Lindsey upstairs in Ethel's house, she asks, "Where's Jace?"

"He came and left. He took the shirt and button with him. I think he's going back to the consignment shop to make sure that Hunter's the one who dropped the shirt off."

"Do you think if they question Hunter, he would tell on his own mother?"

"I don't know. It wouldn't surprise me once he finds out that he could be spending the rest of his life in prison."

Banks leans against the door and asks, "Is there enough proof to charge anyone for anything?"

Lindsey says, "No. Not yet."

"Did Ethel's sister make it?" Piper asks.

"Oh, yes, she did," Lindsay says. "She didn't feel well enough to stay to meet you. They took all of Ethel's pictures, a box of vintage teapots and serving dishes you set off to the side for her, the box of jewelry, and a few other things lying around and left." Piper looks around the room. "She said she'll be in town for another couple days. She said she'll try to be back tomorrow for the auction, but if not, she'll see you later before he leaves town. She asked if you could get a cashier's check made out to her after the auction. She'd like to tie up any lose ends as quickly as possible."

Piper wasn't sure how long it would take for the courts to approve and release the monies collected from the Estate of Ethel Bowers. She hopes Judge Greer will put a rush on it since nothing's tied up in legalities.

"You said 'they.' She wasn't alone?"

Lindsey smiles as if she knows some huge secret. "No, she was with a gentleman."

"Really?"

"Does Maverick Smoker ring a bell?"

Piper's eyes get big. "Wait? Who did you say?"

"I know. It shocked me, too. Looks like we know what his personal reason for wanting to leave was."

Piper looks shocked. "Ethel's sister was with the pub's owner? Are they married?"

"They are. She asked that the cashier check be made out to Abigail Smoker."

"I wonder why she didn't correct me when I was calling her Ms. Bowers on the phone?"

"I think it was because she was dealing with the loss of her sister. She probably wasn't too concerned with the name you were referring to her by."

"Yeah, you're probably right."

Paul and Scott walk upstairs and announce they're done moving the furniture to the garage.

"Thank you both for everything." Piper reaches into her purse to pay them for their work. "I appreciate everything." Piper hands them each two hundred dollars. She knows she'll get paid from the courts for handling Ethel's estate but she isn't sure how much five percent will amount to. She also knows Scott and Paul need their money now. Piper gives Paul a warning look as not to drink up his money.

"Thank you."

Before they leave for the night, Piper says, "Paul, I'll see you back in the morning, right?"

Sundays are usually Paul's day off. He isn't sure whether or not this is his mother's way to make sure he stays sober.

"I'll be here."

"I'll be here, too," Scott says. "I think everyone in Pineapple Grove will be here. Other than Ethel's murder, the auction's the talk of the town."

This makes Piper happy. "Good. Make sure you buy something," Piper teases.

Scott looks around. "Ain't nothing here I want. But Mom and Grandma will be here. I'm afraid I'll be moving all this stuff again."

"What do you mean?"

"Grandma already called me to ask what was going to be in the auction. I'll probably be hauling everything right over to her house by the end of tomorrow night."

Everyone bids farewell and heads home to get ready for the big auction in the morning.

~~~

The turnout for the auction is far more than anyone could have asked for and expected. Banks is forced to park his car nearly a block away. When he walks up to the house, he sees that the auctioneer has already started. Looking at his watch, it's just past eight. He's never known anything to start on time, so this might be a first.

Piper walks around and she's surprised to see most of the townspeople are here since most of the people didn't like Ethel. She's also surprised to see some of the items Mildred's bidding on. Pictures, boxes of miscellaneous items, and kitchen gadgets are some. She's bidding but she isn't winning any of the bids. Maybe it's her way of bidding things up or maybe it's entertaining for her. Stephanie Guest is here with Butcher Bob and his wife. Piper waves "hi" to Sheriff Abbott and Judge Greer. She also sees Harper and suddenly remembers about more boxes of books she found and put off to the side to donate to the library. She puts it to memory to make sure she gets the items before leaving today. By mid-morning, the entire yard is filled with people in lawn chairs bidding on Ethel's prized possessions. The auctioneer was right: There is no way to get this many people in the house.

Later in the day, Hunter and his mom, Ruby, also show up. Piper isn't sure people are here to bid on items or if they're here to socialize and gossip. The items are selling and bringing in big price tags and that's all Piper cares about. Piper's surprised to see Eubanks walking around talking to everyone as if he knows them. He does own the pub so maybe he knows them from there. Of course, if they were patrons of his establishment and he ignored them, the townspeople wouldn't like that. He seems to spend a little
~~~

extra time talking with Mildred, and Piper remembers that Mildred can be a sweet woman when she wants to be. Banks is good looking and she's sure that hasn't gone unnoticed by Mildred. After all, age is just a number, right? Piper takes another close look around the packed space. Does Piper know anyone well enough to know for certain they didn't kill Ethel *or* Carson Eubanks all those years ago? Chills run up her spine just thinking about having a killer among the crowd. She looks at Hunter and Ruby. Is Ruby smart enough to be a mastermind of the killings and is Hunter smart enough to pull it off? Piper thinks not.

She looks around for Jace, but she doesn't see him. He must be following a lead on his own. She wonders if Lindsey knows what's going on. Jace wouldn't miss a day to spend with Lindsey, would he?

At one time or another, Piper has suspected everyone she personally knows in Pineapple Grove of killing Ethel, and now she suspects Hunter and his elderly mother. There's no denying the button belonged to Hunter but what motive did either of them have to kill Ethel?

Lindsey walks up to Piper. "It's a great turnout, huh."

"It sure is."

"I haven't see Abigail or Maverick yet."

"And you won't. Abigail called me this morning and told me they wouldn't make it." Piper looks around the full yard at all of the people. Some are from Pineapple Grove and some people must have come from surrounding areas as Piper's never seen some of them before. "Hard to believe the killer could be right under our noses."

"And we wouldn't even know it."

Piper looks suspiciously at Lindsey and asks, “You didn’t kill Ethel, did you?”

Lindsey’s eyes get big. “No. Did you?”

“Of course not.” Piper thinks for a moment. “But you wouldn’t tell me if you did, would you, Lindsey?”

“Not on your life.”

CHAPTER 8

The auction was a huge success and the auctioneer and Piper couldn't be happier.

The following morning, Piper wakes up and gets ready to begin her day. Now that things are going to be returning back to normal, the feeling is kind of bittersweet. She won't have anything to do with Ethel's place anymore so she'll have some free time. Maybe then she can get back into her photography. The only thing left to do at Ethel's is to call for someone to come and get the rest of the things that didn't sell and to meet up with Abigail and give her the cashier's check. The judge will need to see the receipts from the auctioneer and from the jewelers before this can be done. It's a fairly large sum and Piper's sure Abigail can put it to good use.

The morning news shocks the entire small community of Pineapple Grove. The headline reads, "Newspaper Photographer Questioned in the Murder of Local Resident Ethel Bowers." On the front page are two side-by-side pictures. One photo is of Ethel and the other is a not-so-flattering photo of Hunter.

Lindsey had decided to write up and publish the article in today's paper about Hunter although he did work for the paper and was assigned to be her work photographer. It wasn't an easy decision to make, but Lindsey knew she would be kinder than the other reporters would be when talking about the possible murderer.

The townspeople are in an uproar once the story gets out. This should be good for business at the coffeehouse. One, it'll help clear Piper's name from any wrongdoing, and two, everyone in town will want to get the scoop.

Although Hunter is a suspect, Lindsey still doesn't know the motive. She's hoping that'll be announced in the next few days. Law enforcement officers have been pretty quiet about the evidence. She doesn't know what Hunter's said and what he didn't say. Lindsey's excited to learn more as with each passing day, her newspaper articles will be more interesting as the case builds momentum. This is just the story she was looking for to jumpstart her career in journalism.

Piper and Paul make it to the shop early and start setting up for the day. Paul unlocks the door to the coffeehouse like he always does and Mildred's outside waiting. He wheels her cart for her and they make their way over to the two-top table she has claimed as her own.

Just as Piper suspected, the shop is busy, but Lindsey never made it in. Maybe she didn't want to answer all the questions that she knew would be coming about her photographer, Hunter.

Around ten o'clock, Banks walks through the front door.

"Hey," Piper greets him with a warm friendly smile.

"Hey, yourself."

"I would offer you a seat, but as you can see I don't have any available," Piper says.

"That's all right, I just wanted to stop by and see you."

"Well, here I am,'' she says as she motions her hands from her head all the way down her body to her feet.

He looks at her with appreciation. "Would you want to have dinner with me tonight?"

Piper wonders if this is a date. She hopes it is.

"Sure, I'd love to."

"It'll have to be at the pub. Is that okay?"

"Sure, that's fine."

"It'll also have to be a working date, if you know what I mean? Being the owner, I don't get to take much time off. At least for right now, as I'm still looking for good dependable help."

So, this *is* a date. Sort of.

"I understand and the pub's fine."

Mildred interrupts the conversation and asks for her bill.

"Let me get that for her," Banks says as he fishes out his wallet from his back pocket.

"Thank you, sonny."

He nods. "My pleasure, ma'am."

"Well, looks like I'll have a table for you after all if you want to stick around."

Banks smiles. "I wish I could stay, but I can't." He looks behind him as Mildred still remains seated. "I just stopped by to ask you out. I need to get going so I can open the pub."

"Okay, well, I guess I'll see you tonight then."

"I wanted to ask you out sooner, but I knew you had a lot going on. Maybe now we can get to know each other a little more."

"I'd like that."

Banks smiles his megawatt smile. "Good. Me, too. Does six o'clock work for you?"

"That's perfect."

"I'll see you then." With that he leaves.

Piper walks over to Mildred. "You're leaving kind of early today, Mildred. Is everything okay?"

"Yeah, it's fine. I got a couple things I have to do today."

"Thanks for coming in. I'm sure I'll see you tomorrow."

"God be willin', you'll see me bright and early."

Mildred stands and pulls her cart out of the busy coffeehouse.

The day continues to be a busy one as the townspeople want to know where Lindsey is and what happened with Hunter. Piper hears remarks from her patrons, but she tries to ignore them. She has an uneasy feeling, knowing that Lindsey was working so close to someone who is probably a murderer and never suspected anything.

Just around two o'clock, the door opens and Piper sees a woman whom she's never seen before walking into the coffeehouse. Right behind her is the man she recognized from meeting at Banks' pub. It's Maverick Smoker, so the woman has to be Ethel's sister, Abigail. They take a seat at the table that is usually occupied by Mildred. The shop is almost empty and Piper and Paul are just about to close, but how could she turn away the woman she has been waiting to meet.

Piper walks up to the table and introduces herself.

"You must be Ethel's sister, Abigail."

"I am and this is my husband, Maverick Smoker."

"I'm Piper Armstrong. It's nice to finally meet you."

Piper helps her sit down on the chair.

"You're the one who's in charge of Ethel's estate?" asks Maverick.

"I am," answers Piper.

Maverick looks over at Abigail. "I thought you said her name was Pepper," Maverick says in confusion.

"No. I told you Piper. You must not have been wearing your hearing aid."

"That's because I don't need it. I can hear you just fine now and I'm not wearing it."

Piper laughs inwardly at how cute the old couple fighting is. *I guess the old saying is true about people fighting like an old married couple,* she thinks.

"I was just getting ready to close for the day."

"Oh, I'm sorry. We didn't realize the time," Abigail says, apologetically.

"No, don't be sorry. This is actually the perfect time. I'm glad that we're finally getting the chance to meet and talk. I can put on a fresh pot of coffee if you would like?''

"Decaf for us, please. It's too late in the day for doughnuts."

"Give me one minute, and I'll be right back."

Piper puts on a pot of coffee and informs Paul that he can leave. She turns the "open" sign over to "closed" and then locks the front door. She quickly sends out a text to Lindsey to see if she's all right before pulling up a chair close to Abigail and Maverick.

"So, how has your trip been?"

"Not bad. It was nice to get away for a while, but we're ready to get back home. Pineapple Grove is a beautiful town, but it comes along with a bunch of old memories, many of which we wish to forget," says Abigail.

"That's understandable. The auction did very well and as soon as the judge looks over the receipts from the sales and verifies everything, I should have a cashier's check ready for you sometime tomorrow. Or, if you don't want to wait, I can drive it to you or I could even overnight it if you wanted."

"No, that's fine. We planned on staying for one more day."

Piper smiles as Abigail reminds her of Ethel. "Okay, good. I'm glad you had the chance to come and get some of Ethel's things on Saturday before the auction."

"We didn't take much. We basically just took her photos, some antiques, and her jewelry. We don't really have the space for much else."

"As long as you got what you wanted, I'm happy. I feel like I did my job."

"You did above and beyond, dear. It means a lot to me that you had a memorial service for her."

"You're welcome. I just wanted her to have a proper farewell."

"I'm sure it was lovely. I just wish she wouldn't have been so darn stubborn and just moved away with us when we left. She was determined to find out who killed Carson. It scared the dickens out of me. I wanted no part of any of it. That's why Maverick sold the pub as quickly as he did."

The coffee pot beeps and Piper excuses herself for a second to grab the coffee, some cups, and the cream and sugar.

When she sits back down, Maverick mentions today's paper.

"I see the cops are questioning someone else in Ethel's murder."

“They are. It’s the photographer for the newspaper.”

“I saw he had the same last name as the gal you were asking me about the other day.”

“That’s right. Gallagher.”

Piper still has an uneasy feeling about the police questioning Hunter. She’s not sure they have the whole truth yet. She still thinks the two murders are connected, but she can’t figure out how just yet. There’s no way he could be responsible for Carson’s death. He wasn’t alive back then.

“You said her name was Rudy Gallagher?” Abigail asks.

“No, it’s Ruby with a B. Like the gem.”

Abigail looks over at Maverick. “You told me Rudy, Maverick. I was wondering what woman would be named Rudy.”

Maverick frowns. “Ruby. Rudy. Tomato. Tamato. It all sounds the same to me,” Maverick says.

“Maverick, dear. You have got to start wearing your hearing aid.”

“There’s nothing wrong with my hearing.”

“We’ll talk about this later,” Abigail says.

“Huh? What was that?” Maverick says, cupping his hand up to his ear.

Abigail and Piper just smile.

Abigail says, “I remember a woman named Ruby being at the pub that night Carson was killed. But her last name wasn’t Gallagher, though.”

When Piper spoke with Ruby, she didn't mention she was at the pub the night Carson was killed. Maybe she couldn't remember being there.

"She's been married since then. Her husband sadly died in a car accident."

Abigail thinks long and hard. "If memory serves me, I do believe her name was Ruby Moore. Ethel told me some time ago about her husband. Very tragic."

It's the first time Piper's heard Ruby's maiden name.

"Yes, it is. Do you remember anything else about that night?"

"She was definitely at the pub that night. She was a bit younger than myself, though. Maybe ten years my junior, if my math's right. I always suspected she had a thing for Maverick." Abigail looks adoringly at her now sleeping husband. "You wouldn't know it now, but Maverick here was a stud back in the day."

Piper looks at Maverick and has a hard time picturing he was a ladies' man.

"Was Ruby ever questioned in Carson's murder?"

"No. I don't think so. But people talked back then." *They still do*," Piper thinks to herself. "I never thought it could have been her. Now, her sister was a different story. There was something about her sister that rubbed me the wrong way."

Piper wasn't aware that Ruby had a sister.

"Who's her sister?"

"I think her name was Mildred. Mildred Moore sounds about right."

Pipers mouth falls open. She needs to tread lightly and not say too much. “Ruby has a sister named Mildred?”

Piper didn’t know that Mildred was Ruby’s sister. That makes Hunter and Mildred related.

“Her family called her Milly, but everyone else called her Mildred. Well, they did back in the day. I don’t know what ever happened to her. When Carson died, Maverick sold the pub and we left town. I didn’t want to be around that sort of environment. And my husband was uncomfortable with the attention Ruby was giving him.”

Piper recalls seeing the name Milly on a calendar that Ruby’s guests sign in on at the nursing home. She never thought Milly is Mildred.

“Do you remember anything else about that night?”

“Mildred and Carson had a thing back in the day. I always thought that Mildred was jealous about Ethel and Carson getting married so she poisoned him. Like one of those girls who think if she can’t have him then no one will. She was some character, I tell ya.”

“Was Mildred there that night, too?”

“I remember her being there and leaving early. I think she drugged his drink then left.”

“Did you tell the police what you suspected?”

“Me and everyone else talked to the police that night. Everyone in the pub suspected someone and they were all trying to solve the first murder in Pineapple Grove. It was chaotic that night and there was no way the police could keep up.”

“Why do you say that Mildred drugged Carson?”

"When they questioned her, she said she couldn't have done it because she wasn't there. He died hours after she left." Abigail takes a drink of her hot coffee. Maverick is still sound asleep in the chair. Maybe he can't hear a thing without his hearing aid. "Everyone but me seemed to fall for her story." Abigail looks at her sleeping husband. "I best get him back to the inn."

"Thank you for coming by, and it was nice meeting you."

"The pleasure is mine."

Piper walks with them to the door. "As soon as the judge releases the money from the sale, I'll bring you the cashier's check to the inn."

"Thank you again for all you've done."

"You're welcome."

Lindsey pulls up just as they pull off.

"I've got news."

"Good. So do I."

"Get some coffee so we can talk."

Lindsey sits down and fills her mug with coffee and hazelnut creamer and one sugar. "You go first."

"Ruby's maiden name is Moore."

Lindsey looks at Piper.

"Moore, like in Mildred Moore?" Lindsey asks.

"Yes, they're sisters. When I was at the Forever Young nursing home yesterday and saw the name Milly on the calendar that people sign in on in Ruby's room whenever they visit, I never guessed Milly is actually Mildred."

"Nice. Good detective work. Here's my news." Lindsey sits up straighter in the chair. "I checked into Banks."

"Go on." Piper isn't sure how she feels about this.

"I don't know who his mother is, but I did find that someone we know had a son right around the time that Banks would have been born."

Piper's heart races. "Don't tell me," Piper begins, "It's Mildred?"

"It's Mildred. She gave birth to a son on September twenty-third, which would make her son right around the same age as Banks. I searched but couldn't find anything about her son after that. No father's name, no school records, no anything."

"I have a date with Banks tonight. I should be able to ask him about his childhood then."

"Okay, keep me posted." They both clear off the table. "I wanted to tell you that they didn't arrest Hunter."

"He's free?"

"From what I heard, there wasn't enough evidence to hold him."

"Thanks for the warning."

We're at another dead end, Piper thinks to herself.

On her way home, Piper passes Hunter in the car, and he gives her a dirty look. She tries to ignore the cold chills running down her spine. If looks could kill, Piper would have the starring role of the next funeral in the town of Pineapple Grove.

Piper makes it home and takes Bailey out for a walk before she starts to get ready for her date tonight. The thought of having to ask Banks such personal information isn't sitting well with her. How can she tell him that people think his mother killed his father at the pub all those years ago? Maybe she won't mention it.

She decides on a little red and white dress with white heels. Although this may feel like an interrogation, it's still a date. Or at least the closest thing to a date that Piper's had in a very long time.

Her mind races on the drive to the pub. Once she gets her thoughts together, she decides that this has to be the time. She gets out of her car and makes her way inside the pub. When she walks in, Banks is at the front door waiting.

"Perfect timing." Banks looks her up and down. "You look beautiful."

Piper blushes. "Thank you."

"I ended up finding someone to cover for me. I thought we could sit outside under the umbrella and have dinner if that's all right."

"Sounds lovely."

He takes her by the hand and leads her through the darkened pub to the outside river view seating area.

"This okay?" he asks, pointing to a table in the center of the patio. Banks knows he's with the most beautiful woman in Pineapple Grove and he wants others to see him with her.

"I was actually hoping we could sit somewhere a little more private."

That's even better, Banks thinks to himself. "Very well then." He leads her to the most intimate table on the patio. "This private enough for you?"

"It's perfect. Thank you."

He pulls out her chair before taking a seat himself.

"I'm hoping we can use this time to get to know each other a little better."

That's exactly what Piper wants. "Sounds great."

The server comes over and Banks orders a bottle of champagne and an appetizer. Banks notices that Piper isn't her usual self. "Are you okay?"

"They didn't arrest Hunter. I passed him leaving the coffeehouse, and the look he gave me sent chills down my spine."

Banks looks concerned. "Did he say anything?"

"No, I was in my car and he was in his. It was just a look, but I got cold chills from it."

"I imagine he's still upset about being a suspect."

"I suppose so."

The drinks and appetizers come. "So, Piper, tell me something about yourself."

"What do you want to know?"

"Everything."

"It may take longer than one date." Piper giggles.

"Then we'll have as many as it takes."

"I'm divorced. The mother of two grown children, Hannah and Paul, and a white poodle named Bailey." Piper takes a sip of her champagne. "Your turn."

"Never been married. No kids."

Getting information from Banks may be easier than Piper thought.

“I know about your dad, but what about your mother?”

“That’s a long story.”

Piper leans back as if she’s relaxing. “I have time.”

“My mother lives here in town. That’s actually one of the reasons why I came back to Pineapple Grove.”

“Oh, do I know her?”

“You do. She was in your shop earlier today. Mildred Moore.”

“Mildred’s your mother?” Piper says.

“That’s right. I was going to tell you, but it never came up.”

“But your father raised you, didn’t he?”

“He did. My father told me that right after Mom gave birth to me, he took me and left. He brought me back here when I was ten to live with him, then I left Pineapple Grove again when I was eighteen to join the military.”

“And you just returned back here again a few months ago?”

“Yes, that right.”

“Did you know who your mother was?”

“No. He told me my mother died while giving birth.”

“I’m sorry.”

“I’m sure he had his reasons for telling such an outlandish lie.”

“Mildred was young when she gave birth.”

“She was. It was very hard on her. She dropped out of school and was home schooled during her pregnancy. Her family was embarrassed that she was unwed and pregnant. Things were a lot different back then."

"I'm sure."

The server comes and they both order a light meal. With such a heavy and deep conversation, a heavy meal won't sit well with either.

"I guess since your dad was dating Ethel, Mildred and Ethel knew about each other."

"Mom loved my dad. She always had. She was angry when Dad left and took me away from her."

"I can imagine."

Piper wonders if Mildred was upset enough to kill Ethel and Carson.

"You don't think Mom killed my dad and Ethel, do you?"

Should I tell him the truth? "No. I'm just saddened over your story, that's all." It's not a total lie. "I like Mildred. I see her nearly every day. It makes me sad to know she has a son and wasn't able to see him."

"We've stayed in touch since I was eighteen years old."

"How did you learn she was your mother?"

"On my eighteenth birthday, my dad told me, then Mildred confirmed the story."

"Yet she never mentioned you to me or to anyone else."

"She didn't want anyone to know. She lived here and it was her wish so I agreed."

"Why did you stay with Ethel when you came back and not with your mom?"

“Ethel and I are still friends. I had no reason to not like her. Mom didn’t have any extra room in her one-bedroom apartment and when Ethel offered, I accepted. Mom knew and she seemed to be fine with it.”

“Wow. This is very shocking to hear.”

Mildred had the means and she had a motive to kill Carson — and Ethel for that matter. Piper can’t wait to get back to tell Lindsey what she found out.

“Can we talk about something else?” Banks asks.

“Yes, please.”

They have dinner and she tell Banks how long she’s been in Pineapple Grove. The rest of the conversation is light and uplifting. Before she leaves, he asks her out again and she gladly accepts.

On the way home, Piper calls Lindsey and tells her that Banks was forthcoming about his childhood and that he confirmed what they already knew: Mildred is his mother.

“Mildred has a motive to kill Carson senior and Ethel,” Lindsey whispers.

“I know. But I don’t want Banks to know until we know for sure she killed them.”

“I understand, but we need to talk to Mildred.”

“We need to talk to Hunter, too, and find out why his button was in Ethel’s house. Piper looks at the clock on the dashboard. “I’ll pick you up in ten.”

“I’ll be ready.”

They knock on the door of Mildred’s place and wait for an answer.

"What do you want?" she asks, wearing an old housecoat.

"Mildred, can we talk?"

Seeing how serious they look, she opens the door wide for them to enter. "I suppose you won't leave until we do."

Mildred has overheard enough to guess that they suspect her of murder.

"Thank you," Piper says.

"Can I get you some coffee?"

"No, thank you," answers Piper almost too fast.

"I guess I can't say I blame you. But I would never poison either one of you." Mildred nearly falls down into the large soft chair. "What is it? What do you want?"

"I was just talking to your son, Banks."

"God, please leave him out of this. He's been through enough."

Piper and Lindsey sit down. Piper leans forward. "We know you killed Carson and Ethel."

"Can't you just let it go? They're gone and the world is a better place without them."

"Why did you do it?"

"Carson Eubanks got me pregnant and left me when I needed him the most. He knew I was going to have his baby, but he was more concerned with Ethel than he was with his own family. Back in those days, if you did get someone knocked up out of wedlock you got married and raised your family. You took care of business. Carson, my son's father, made me look like the town whore. He wanted absolutely nothing to do with me." Mildred inhales deeply.

"If I had family out of town, I would have moved in with them, had my baby, and raised him with their help."

Lindsey wipes away a tear. "I'm sorry, Mildred."

Mildred waves a hand to dismiss the sentiment.

"When I told him that I wouldn't be able to raise a child alone, and I would have to give it up for adoption, we came to the agreement that I would hide the pregnancy as best I could and give birth in another state and when the baby came he would take it away and raise it. Alone. He had the means to give our child a good life. That's all I wanted for my son." Mildred wipes away a tear. "He didn't hold his end of the bargain. He moved back when my son was ten to be with *that* woman. He told everyone his child's mother died during childbirth. I had to watch my son grow up and not say anything to him. Can you imagine what that was like for me?" Piper and Lindsey are both crying. "That was the hardest thing I've ever had to do. Well, one of the hardest things I ever had to do. Once Banks was eighteen, old enough to know about his mother, Carson told him about me and that only made it worse. That's when Banks decided to move away and join the service and that's when I snapped. Carson and Ethel got engaged, and that was the last straw for me."

"You never talked to your son after he joined the service?"

"I did. He wrote me and told me his reasoning to join. I thought it was to get away from me, but it wasn't. He decided long before he was eighteen he wanted to serve his country. Finding out about me was just bad timing. He had actually joined the service while still in high school when he was seventeen years old."

"And you wrote to him while he was away?"

"We wrote back and forth." Mildred smiles proudly. "I attended his graduation and we'd see each other during his leave times. We grew close during his enlistment."

"What happened with Carson and Ethel?"

"He didn't love me, and he certainly never respected me. He took my only child. He brought him back and flaunted my son in front of my face when he knew I couldn't and wouldn't say anything. I had to protect my son from being ridiculed. I couldn't take watching the man I once loved marry the person who ruined my family and my life. I waited a long time to get her, and I finally did."

"Help me to understand something."

"Lord, I'm tired of hiding this. What do you want to know?"

"So, you poisoned Carson the night at the pub?"

"I did and then I left in a hurry. He was pretty drunk and never even tasted that his drink was laced with rat poison."

Lindsey asks, "So how did you kill Ethel?"

"That took some time. She didn't drink alcohol so I had to do it more slowly so she couldn't taste the pesticide."

"Her coffee was poisoned. How did you manage that?"

Piper prays that Mildred didn't poison any of the coffee in the local businesses, especially her coffeehouse.

"I poisoned her personal coffee stash at her house. She didn't entertain so I knew no one else would be at risk of drinking the poison but her."

"How did you get in her house to do that?"

"When Banks came back in town, I didn't have any room in my apartment, and I knew he and Ethel were close. So, when she asked him to stay in her spare duplex I knew it was my chance."

"What do you mean?"

"He had a house key, and he told me it was for all the exterior doors to the house. One day I took the key and made a copy of it. I used the copied key to enter her house. That's when I laced the bag of coffee beans I found in the freezer with the rat poisoning."

Piper knows people often keep coffee in the freezer for freshness.

Piper considers this and finds it unsettling.

"If you and Ethel were feuding, why would she make you executor of her estate?"

"Out of spite. To rub salt in my wound, if you will."

Piper looks at Lindsey. This is going to be tough.

"I don't agree with what you've done, but what's done is done."

"Are you going to turn me in?"

"No. *We're not.*"

Mildred knew that was too good to be true.

"You want me to turn myself in?

"I think you have to. What other choice do you have?"

Mildred thinks about what her choices are. She thinks the better choice would be to leave and go to some tropical island and live out the last of her days on sandy beaches with a fruity cocktail in her hand. But Piper has other ideas.

“Would it be okay if I did it tomorrow? I need to tie up some loose ends with my son.”

“I think it’s best he hears it from you.”

“Thank you. I’ll turn myself in to Sheriff Abbott first thing in the morning and tell him what I’ve done.”

“And what about Banks?”

“I’ll call him this evening and ask him to come over. What I have to say will need to be said in person.”

“I agree.”

“Piper, I’ve always liked you. My son may need someone to help him get through this, and I hope you’ll be understanding of his needs.”

“Mildred, I’ll do my best.”

“You both should come over for breakfast in the morning. It’ll be my farewell breakfast.”

“Are you sure, Mildred?” Lindsey asks.

“Absolutely. Be here around seven o’clock. We’ll eat together before I turn myself in.”

“Okay, we’ll be here. We can also go with you when you turn yourself in if you want.”

“Will it make it any easier?”

Lindsey shakes her head. “I doubt it.”

“It might be nice having someone there with me.”

They bid farewell and get into the car.

“Case solved,” Piper announces.

“Two cases solved, you mean.”

Piper looks over with a smile. “We did just crack two murder cases.”

“That we did, but there’s still something we don’t know.”

“What’s that?”

“How Hunter’s button got in Ethel’s house.”

“Let’s ask him.”

Piper drives while Lindsey calls Hunter. “We need to talk. I’m coming over.”

“I’m not home.”

“Where are you? I’ll come there.”

“Visiting Mom.”

“Stay put. I’ll be there in a few.”

The ride to the nursing home is a quiet one. Both are thinking about what they will say to Ruby and Hunter. They already have the truth, but they need to tie up some loose ends. Piper’s also thinking about Banks and Mildred. It won’t be easy for him to hear what his mother’s done.

When they make it inside the nursing home, Lindsey knocks on the door and waits for Ruby to invite them into her room.

Ruby’s in bed with a blanket pulled up to her chest and Hunter’s sitting beside the bed in a chair. He’s wearing a bright yellow shirt. Almost too bright of a color for any man to wear.

“What can I do for you?” Ruby asks.

“We want to talk to you about your sister, Mildred.”

“What about her?”

“We’re trying to figure out why you and Hunter are covering up for her,” Lindsey says.

Piper has no idea what she’s talking about. She decides to let Lindsey do the talking.

“Why do you think we’re covering anything up?’’

“We just talked to Mildred and she confessed about killing Carson and Ethel.”

“Sounds like something for the police to investigate.”

“They will tomorrow.” Ruby and Hunter look at each other. When neither says anything, Lindsey decides they need to believe this isn’t a bluff, although it is. “We know about the rat poison in Carson’s drink at the pub. We know about Ethel’s coffee being poisoned.” Still they remain silent. “We also know about Carson and Mildred’s son, Banks.” Lindsey lets that sink in before saying more. “We know that Carson took him at birth to raise as a single father. We know that Carson told everyone that his son’s mother died while giving birth.”

Ruby cries. “He was a rat. Who would do that? My sister suffered for many years because of him.”

“We don’t agree with what he did to her. It was very cruel.”

Hunter speaks up. “My aunt’s too old to be going to prison. I told my mother I’d look after her before she died, and I’m trying to keep my promise.”

Lindsey looks over at Hunter. “They called you in for questioning in Ethel’s murder,” Lindsey says.

“You should know, you wrote the article about it.”

“It was either me or one of those other reporters.”

“Why did it have to be you?”

"I offered. I thought I could be more sensitive when writing the article about you than the other reporters. If you had read the article you would have saw I did my best to not make you look too guilty."

"Thank you, I guess."

"But they didn't charge you?"

"There was no evidence. Thankfully, the morning Ethel died I had been at the *Times* working since four o'clock that morning. My boss verified that I was there and Sheriff Abbott let me go. I can't leave town or anything like that in case they need me for more questioning."

"We know the button they found at Ethel's was yours."

"And how can you know that?"

"Because you donated the shirt with the missing button to the consignment shop and we went and bought it."

Ruby hits her son on the arm.

Piper asks, "How did you explain the button to the sheriff?"

"I told them I moved some furniture for Ethel before she passed and I must have lost it then."

"And since Ethel kept an impeccably clean house, we know the button wasn't there for long. In fact, we know the button was lost after Ethel died."

No one answers.

"You might as well tell us. We already know the truth." Lindsey was getting good at this interrogation line of questioning. She didn't know why he was there, but she was about to find out the truth.

"Yeah, I went into Ethel's."

"Why?"

"To get rid of the evidence."

Lindsey suspects there's only two things that could be used as evidence. Coffee and poison. Since most people have pesticides in their home, she's making an educated guess it was the poisoned coffee. Since the sheriff probably took the coffee and anything related to it as evidence, she's not sure what coffee Hunter could have taken.

"You took the coffee?"

"The coffee pot and coffee grinder was already gone when I got there."

Piper and Lindsey suspect the police took those items as evidence.

"But the coffee still there?"

"I took the only coffee I found in the freezer in a zip lock bag. A lot of people don't know that keeps your coffee fresher longer. While I was there searching the place, my shirt got caught on a drawer pull and it must have popped my button."

"How did you get in? There weren't any signs of forced entry," Lindsey asks.

If Hunter was smart, he would remain silent.

Ruby says, "He used a key."

Piper and Lindsey know that it must have been the same key Mildred made a copy of from Banks' key ring.

Ruby wipes away a tear. "What'll happen now?"

"Mildred said she'll turn herself in to the sheriff in the morning. She's calling her son to come over this evening so she can confess to him first."

"I never agreed with my sister, but I saw her level of hurt. The two deserved what they got."

Piper doesn't know if anyone ever deserves death as a punishment.

"I'm sure the police will be in touch," Lindsey says. "If I were you, I wouldn't speak to anyone else about this."

"Do my son and I need an attorney?" Ruby asks.

"If you keep talking, you will."

Before leaving, Piper says, "Your memory seems to be clearer today than it was the last time we spoke."

Ruby takes Lindsey's advice and remains quiet. She just watches as Lindsey and Piper walk out of her room.

Piper knows Ruby's "dementia" was a fake.

On the way home Piper asks Lindsey, "How did you know all of that?"

"Some of it I didn't. It was a bluff."

"You're good at that."

"I know."

Piper drops off Lindsey before heading home. She feels bad for Banks and what he must be going through. Mildred said her son had been through enough. Losing his father to murder and now losing his mother to a lifetime in prison is a lot for anyone to deal with. Piper wishes she had the words to help him through this, but she doesn't.

~~~
~~~

Mildred's tired and ready to put all of this to an end. She'd rather go straight to jail than have to tell her only child that she's killed his father and his father's mistress nearly three decades apart.

She calls Banks and asks him to come over whenever he can. Although she doesn't make it sound like it is an emergency, he wastes no time getting there.

He knocks before using his key to enter the house.

"Is everything okay?" he asks, walking into the well-lit living room.

"It's fine. I didn't expect to see you so soon."

"The pub was slow. Amy's going to close for me." He takes a seat beside his mother on the couch. "What's going on?"

"I have something to tell you."

The look on her face tells him it's important and possibly not good news.

"Are you sick?"

"Some people might think so."

"Do you have cancer?"

Mildred smiles. "No, Banks. I'm not ill."

"Then what is it?"

"It's about your father." Banks remains quiet. There's no other way for Mildred to say it. "I killed him and Ethel."

"That's not funny."

"It's true. I'm responsible for killing your father."

"And Ethel?"

"Her, too."

He rests his elbows on his knees and clasps his hands together. "I don't understand."

"You already know the circumstances that led to you being raised by your father. But you don't know the entire story. We agreed that he would stay gone until your eighteenth birthday. Then when you were eighteen he would bring you back and we both would tell you the truth. I wanted you to be old enough to understand and I hoped you'd be forgiving." Mildred wipes away a tear. "But he came back when you were ten years old. He never said the reason, but I think he came back because of Ethel. He flaunted her in front of me, but that wasn't the worst part. She started acting as your mother, and I had to sit back and watch that. You were always the most important person to me. That's why I gave you away. Because I couldn't give you the life you needed, the life you deserved."

"I understand that and I know how hard it must have been for you."

"Do you, really?"

"I do. I can't imagine ever having to make a choice like that. You should know that I had a good life."

Mildred smiles. "I could see that and that's all I ever wanted. But for your father to bring you back sooner than we agreed on, was cruel. It tore me up to have to see you day in and day out and not be able to tell you who I was. I used to sit outside the school and watch you play on the playground."

"I never knew that."

"I know you didn't, but Ethel did. She saw me lurking in the background just trying to get a glimpse of you."

"I'm sorry, Mom."

"It wasn't your fault."

"I watched as Ethel picked you up from school and walked you home. She knew I was watching and she would kiss you and look over at me and smile. I spent eight years watching and begging your father to spare my feelings and leave. But he wouldn't."

"Then when I was eighteen and learned you were my mother, I had already enlisted in the service." He runs his hands through his hair. "I can't imagine how that made you feel."

Mildred smiles. "Proud. That's how I felt. My heart was full that my only son was defending our country."

"You always wrote me, sent me care packages, and you never missed any of my graduations."

"We bonded during that time."

"We did and I'm thankful for that time."

"Me, too."

"After you left, I asked your father why he returned before our agreed time. Why would he torture me like that?"

"What did he say?"

"He laughed. He laughed right in my face." Mildred wipes away a tear. "I couldn't take it anymore. I was going to make him pay, and I was going to make Ethel pay, too."

"You're the one who poisoned him that night at the pub? The night before he was to marry Ethel?"

"I did. He was drunk, and I slid a deadly dose of rat poison into his drink. I then went home and waited."

"And Ethel?"

"I wanted to kill her that night, too, but it wasn't that easy."

"You held a grudge all this time?"

"I did."

"How did you do it?"

"I poisoned her coffee. I had to make sure it was done slowly. Your dad was so drunk he never tasted it, but Ethel, she never drank. She'd be able to tell something was off."

"Did you poison the coffee at the local businesses?"

"No. Of course not. I poisoned her coffee at her house."

"Why are you telling me this?"

"Piper and Lindsey figured it out."

"They're not turning you in, are they?"

"No."

"Good."

"I'm turning myself in, in the morning."

"What? Why? I have some money. We can leave tonight."

Mildred touches his hand lightly. "I'm tired, sonny. It's time for me to come clean and put everything behind me."

"I understand." Banks wipes away his tears with the backs of his band. "I feel like we didn't have enough time together."

"It's not over. Maybe they'll see I did a justice to the community and will order me to community service?"

Banks and Mildred both know that's wishful thinking.

"Are you going to be okay?" Banks asks, taking his mother's frail hand in his.

"Me? Don't be silly. I'll be just fine. I'll have three meals a day, free medical, and free room and board. It's what every senior citizen should get after the age of sixty." Banks agrees that all of our senior citizens deserve all of those things, plus their freedom. "I'm going to have a cup of coffee and turn in for the night."

"When are you turning yourself into the sheriff's department?"

"I told Piper I would do it first thing in the morning. I invited her and Lindsey here for breakfast. We'll eat and then I'll turn myself in."

"What time?"

"Around seven."

Banks nods. "I'll spend the night and I'll make breakfast. I'll go with you when you turn yourself in to the sheriff in the morning."

"You're going to cook breakfast?"

He wants to laugh. He owns a restaurant and a pub. Is it hard to believe that he cooks from time to time? "I thought I would."

"Good. I get to sleep in. Wake me up when it's ready." She drinks one last cup of coffee before she turns in for the night. "I love you, Banks."

He holds her in a firm embrace and kisses the top of her head.

"I love you, too, Mom." Before she goes to bed, Banks moves her wheeled cart out of the way and closer to the wall. The cart seems heavy to pull. He suspects maybe the wheels need oiled. As soon as he picks up her crochet bag from the cart, he knows why. The bag is heavier than a bag containing yarn and crocheting needles should be because inside the bag is a brick. "What are you doing with this?" he asks, holding up the heavy brick.

"That's my protection."

"Protection? From what?"

"Would-be muggers."

"And this is going to protect you?"

"After I hit him with it, it will."

Banks shakes his head. If it makes her feel safer, so be it.

"Good night, Mom."

She looks back at her only son. "Good night, sonny."

~~~

Just as Piper's about to turn in, her cell phone rings from an unknown number. She immediately looks at the clock and wonders if it's Paul. Not likely since he's in bed for work tomorrow. "Piper speaking."

"It's Banks."

"Hi."

"Mom just drank a cup of coffee and went to bed."

"Did you guys talk?"

"She told me everything."

"I'm sorry."

"I told Mom I'd go with her in the morning to the sheriff's office, and I don't want to leave her here alone."
~~~

“I’ll be right over to sit with you.”

“Are you sure?”

“I need to change so give me a few minutes.”

“Thanks, Piper. I appreciate it.”

“You’re welcome.”

Piper wakes up Paul and tells him he’ll need to open the coffeehouse without her. He grumbles, says a few mumbled words, and rolls over on his side. She dresses in yoga pants and a tee and heads over to Mildred’s to meet Banks. He’s waiting at the door for her.

“What a night.” He runs his hands through his thick hair.

“I’m sorry.”

Piper walks into the house and notices a coffee cup sitting on the coffee table. Beside the wall is Mildred’s shopping cart that once belonged to Ethel. There’s yarn and a knitting needle sticking out of the cart.

Piper and Banks stay up talking until morning about what this will mean for Mildred. Piper must have dosed off because when she wakes up on the couch, Banks is cooking breakfast. Piper folds the throw blanket that had been covering her and tosses it on the arm of the chair.

Just before seven o’clock, Lindsey knocks on the door and Banks lets her in.

“Breakfast is almost done,” he says, opening the door for Lindsey.

Lindsey looks over at Piper. “Have you been here all night?”

“I called her over to sit with me last night.”

“How’s your mom?”

“She’s still asleep. I’ll wake her in a minute.”

Piper and Lindsey know that Mildred’s an early riser as she’s always at the coffeehouse bright and early.

“Coffee?’ he asks.

Piper quickly shakes her head. She may never drink coffee again after last night.

“No, thank you,” Lindsey answers.

“Maybe I should have made tea,” he says, walking into the kitchen.

Piper picks up Mildred’s coffee cup from last night to take to the kitchen to rinse out when she smells a strange odor coming from it. She raises the cup to her nose and breathes in. She isn’t sure but she’s fearful that the smell is some sort of pesticide.

“Banks?”

He pokes his head around the corner. “What is it?”

“This is your mother’s coffee cup, right?”

“Yes, she drank her coffee in that cup last night.”

“Did you have any coffee last night?”

“No. Why?” He walks into the living room. “What’s up?”

“Does this smell funny to you?”

Piper, Lindsey, and Banks make eye contact in turn when he realizes that his mother may have poisoned herself.

He takes the cup and smells it before they all run upstairs to check on Mildred. Either she isn’t breathing or her breathing is very shallow. Banks touches his mother gently, but her skin is grey and cold. Mildred Moore had died in her sleep.

Banks sits on the bed, taking his mother's hand in hers. "My mother took her own life."

"I'm sorry, Banks," Piper says.

"She did it last night. I was right there while she sipped her coffee, and I had no idea it was poison."

"Don't blame yourself for this," Lindsey says. "It must have been her plan all along."

"Why would you say that?"

"Because she kept the rat poison for something. She already had her mind made up."

"I suppose so. What do we do now?"

Piper says, "We need to call the police."

"What will we tell them?" he asks.

"That your mother passed away in her sleep."

"And what she did to my dad and Ethel."

"What about them? Your poor mother is in her seventies. She must have died of natural causes. I don't see any reason to tell the police anything else," Piper says. "What good will it do to tell the police? We don't have proof and the only witness can't testify or admit it."

Lindsey agrees.

Banks thinks this through. He knows his Aunt Ruby and Hunter won't say anything. No one needs to know what his mother did. Pineapple Grove will just file this case as another unsolved murder. It'll be another cold case file. This could work, but there's only one problem.

He looks over at Lindsey. “This could be just the story you’re looking for, Lindsey.”

“What? That Mildred Moore died in her sleep. Doesn’t sound too interesting to me.”

Lindsey knows that Banks is talking about a double homicide/suicide story. It would be the story she’s looking for, but at whose expense? This is one story that doesn’t need told.

Banks washes the coffee cup before he calls the police. After they arrive, they call the medical examiner to come and get his mother’s body.

Later that day, Piper meets with the judge, and he approves the receipts of the estate sale and the bank issues Piper two cashier’s checks. One is made out to Abigail Smoker and the other is issued to Piper for serving as executor of Ethel Bowers’ estate. Piper is surprised at the amount of both checks. She gives some to Lindsey for helping her and gives a little extra to Paul and Scott for their hard work with moving the heavy furniture in Ethel’s house. She isn’t sure what her plans are for the rest but she will put it to good use. Maybe she’ll invest some in her photography hobby.

When Piper and Banks take Abigail and Maverick the check from Ethel’s estate sale, Abigail hands Piper a letter that they found behind one of the pictures they took from Ethel’s house. The letter is addressed to Mildred from Ethel.

“I found this behind a picture I got from Ethel’s. I thought you could give it to Mildred the next time you see her.”

“Thank you, I will.” Piper takes the letter.

Mildred died this morning but the news of her death hasn't been announced to the public yet.

Once outside, Piper gives the letter to Banks. Not everyone in Pineapple Grove knows he is Mildred's son. That's his secret and if he wants to tell it, it is up to him.

Banks doesn't open the letter but takes it back to Piper's coffeeshop.

When they get out of the car, Piper asks, "Are you going to read it?"

Banks considers this.

"What good could come from it?"

"Good point."

"Both parties are now dead and the feud between them needs to end."

Piper watches as he takes a lighter from his jean pocket and puts a flame to the sealed envelope. They watch it burn until there is nothing more than ash that blows away with the wind. The feud is now over and everything in Pineapple Grove will return to normal. Or would it?

THE END

To continue reading more about the characters in the Pineapple Grove Cozy Murder Mystery Series, watch for *Murder in the Library* featuring the same characters you have grown to love and some new ones.

BOOKS BY BRENDA KENNEDY AND KAYDEN KEATON

COZY MYSTERY BOOKS WRITTEN BY BRENDA KENNEDY AND KAYDEN KEATON

Book One: *Murder Behind the Coffeehouse*

Book Two: *Murder in the Library…* coming soon

ROMANCE BOOKS BY BRENDA KENNEDY

We support Indie Authors. If you read this book, please take the time to go to the purchasing site and give it a review.

Independent authors count on your reviews to get the word out about our books. Thank you for taking the time to read my books and taking the extra time to review them. I appreciate it very much.

Disclaimer: People and places in this book have been used fictitiously and without malice.

The Forgotten Trilogy

Book One: *Forgetting the Past* (Free)

Book Two: *Living for Today*

Book Three: *Seeking the Future*

The Learning to Live Trilogy

Book One: *Learning to Live* (Free)

Book Two: *Learning to Trust*

Book Three: *Learning to Love*

The Starting Over Trilogy

Book One: *A New Beginning*

Book Two: *Saving Angel*

Book Three: *Destined to Love*

The Freedom Trilogy

Book One: *Shattered Dreams*

Book Two: *Broken Lives*

Book Three: *Mending Hearts*

The Fighting to Survive Trilogy

Round One: *A Life Worth Fighting*

Round Two: *Against the Odds*

Round Three: *One Last Fight*

The Rose Farm Trilogy

Book One: *Forever Country*

Book Two: *Country Life*

Book Three: *Country Love*

Books in the Seashell Island Stand-alone Series

Book One: *Home on Seashell Island* (Free)

Book Two: *Christmas on Seashell Island*

Book Three: *Living on Seashell Island*

Book Four: *Moving to Seashell Island*

Book Five: *Returning to Seashell Island*

Books in the Montgomery Wine Stand-alone Series

Book One: *A Place to Call Home*

Stand-alone books in the "Another Round of Laughter Series" written by Brenda and some of her siblings: Carla Evans, Martha Farmer, Rosa Jones, and David Bruce

Cupcakes Are Not a Diet Food (Free)

Kids Are Not Always Angels

Aging Is Not for Sissies

ACKNOWLEDGEMENTS

To Brenda's husband, Rex: Who would have known where this journey has taken us? Thank you for supporting me in following my dreams. Thank you for giving me the freedom to spread my wings and catching me when I fall. Thank you for always believing in me. You are my partner for life, and I love you.

Brenda's children: Thank you for reminding me what is important every single day. I love you.

Brenda's grandchildren: Thank you for reminding me that I am somebody; I am your grandma and nothing else matters. I love you all.

Brenda's sisters and brothers: Thank you for your endless support. I love you.

Brenda's brother David: Without you, I wouldn't have been able to publish the first book. Thank you for making my ideas better and for all you do. Editing, proofreading, polishing, formatting, ideas, articles, and research websites. See, I do pay attention. Thank you. Thank you for pushing me until I get it right. Maybe someday I'll learn the right place to put the commas. I love you and I can never thank you enough.

Brenda's daughter, Carleen. Thank you for doing the final read through. I love your keen eye. The red pen and highlighter, not so much. You make my books awesome. Thank you and I love you.

Becki Angle Martin: Thank you for designing this stunning cover. You saw our vision and brought it to life. Thank you. We're proud to call you family.

To our readers: Thank you for reading and reviewing our books.

For those readers who enjoy a darker, more intense read: Brenda's daughter Carleen Jamison has published her debut novel, which is titled *Inappropriate Reactions*. It is Book One of the Mind Games Series. This book is intended for mature audiences only and is available on all leading online eBookstore platforms. You can follow her on her Smashwords Author's page:

https://www.smashwords.com/profile/view/carleenjamison

Info for David Bruce, Brenda's Brother

David writes collections of anecdotes such as *The Funniest People in Movies*, and he retells classics in such books as William Shakespeare*'s 38 Plays*: *Retellings in Prose*. His books can be found for sale on all leading online electronic book sale platforms. He is apparently either the first or second person in the world to translate all 38 of William Shakespeare's plays into today's English. He may also be the first person in the world to translate at least three of Ben Jonson's plays into today's English.

ABOUT THE AUTHORS

Kayden Keaton is a son of Brenda Kennedy. This is his pen name as he wishes to remain anonymous. It's hard, but she's trying her best to keep his secret. He is currently setting up social media pages for his readers to follow his adventure in writing. And he's sure this will be an adventure you won't want to miss. He currently resides in Ohio with his extended family.

Brenda Kennedy, an award-winning and bestselling author, is a true believer of romance. Her stories are based on the relationships that define our lives—compassionate, emotionally gripping, and uplifting novels with true-to-life characters that stay with her readers long after the last page is turned.

Her varied, not always pleasant, background has given her the personal experience to take her readers on an emotional, sometimes heart-wrenching, journey through her stories. Brenda has been a struggling single mom, a survivor of domestic abuse, waitress, corrections officer, hostage negotiator, and corrections nurse. She is also a wife, mom, and grandmother. Even though her life was not always rainbows and butterflies, she is a survivor and believes her struggles have made her the person she is today.

Brenda is the author of the award-winning book *Forever Country*(The Rose Farm Trilogy Book 1, for Best Book in Series). She has been dubbed "The Queen of Cliffhangers" by her adoring readers because books one and two in her trilogies almost always have a cliffhanger ending. In Brenda's own words, "I write series that end in cliffhangers, because I love them. I always give away the first book in each cliffhanger series so you have nothing to lose by reading it."

As of recently, Brenda's started branching out and writing standalone books. However, she currently has a cliffhanger trilogy brewing her head and she can't wait to start writing it.

Her books have appeared on the *Publishers Weekly* Top 25 Best-Sellers list eleven times—once she had four titles on the list at the same time—along with Amazon, iBooks, and Barnes and Noble rankings in the top 100 books in contemporary romance.

Brenda moved to sunny Florida in 2006 and never looked back. She loves freshly squeezed lemonade, crushed ice, teacups, wine glasses, non-franchise restaurants, ice cream cones, boating, picnics, cookouts, throwing parties, lace, white wine, mojitos, strawberry margaritas, white linen tablecloths, fresh flowers, lace, mountains, oceans, and Pinterest. She also loves to read and write and to spend time with her family.

You may follow her on:

FB author page: http://on.fb.me/1ywRwmI

BookBub Author's Page:
https://www.bookbub.com/authors/brenda-kennedy

GoodReads: http://bit.ly/1szWiw5

Twitter: https://twitter.com/BrendaKennedy_

Webpage: http://brendakennedyauthor.com

www.ingramcontent.com/pod-product-compliance
Ingram Content Group UK Ltd.
Pitfield, Milton Keynes, MK11 3LW, UK
UKHW041855190726
13854UKWH00002B/921